# Francis Bacon's Armchair

# Sébastien Brebel

# *Francis Bacon's Armchair*

A Novel
Translated by Jesse Anderson

 **DALKEY ARCHIVE PRESS**

Despite its mission to support French literature in translation, and in particular to to support the cause and well-being of translators, CNL (Centre national du livre) would not provide support for the translator of this book, and this at a time when there has been a substantial decrease in the number of books being translated into English. Dalkey Archive urges CNL to return to its mission of aiding translators.

Originally published in French as *Le Fauteuil de Bacon* by P.O.L in 2007.

Library of Congress Cataloging-in-Publication Data

Names: Brebel, Sebastien, author. | Anderson, Jesse, 1987- translator.
Title: Francis Bacon's armchair / by Sebastien Brebel ; translated by Jesse
   Anderson.
Other titles: Fauteuil de Bacon. English
Description: Victoria, TX : Dalkey Archive Press, 2016. | "Originally
   published in French as Le Fauteuil de Bacon in 2007  . . . P.O.L Editeur"
   [Paris] -- Verso title page.
Identifiers: LCCN 2015045368 | ISBN 9781943150014 (pbk. : alk. paper)
Subjects: LCSH: Psychological fiction.
Classification: LCC PQ2702.R42 F3813 2016 | DDC 843/.92--dc23
LC record available at http://lccn.loc.gov/2015045368

Publication of this book was made possible by the Illinois Arts Council, a state agency, and the Florence J. Gould Foundation. This book is supported by the Institut Français (Royaume-Uni) as part of the Burgess programme.

www.dalkeyarchive.com
Victoria, TX / McLean, IL / London / Dublin

Dalkey Archive Press publications are, in part, made possible through the support of the University of Houston-Victoria and its programs in creative writing, publishing, and translation.

Printed on permanent / durable acid-free paper

# Francis Bacon's Armchair

Just yesterday (that is to say: a certain time ago) I was imagining a new life for myself, and in this new life that I was imagining (just yesterday), I decided that my bedroom would play an important and necessary role. The bedroom was modest, suitably furnished (nothing more), and my first impression upon entering it was that I shouldn't touch a thing. I walked several steps further into the bedroom and immediately understood that I shouldn't think of it as my own, should not think of here (or rather there) (in this imaginary bedroom) as my home. There would be no need to think about changing the layout of the bedroom, nor would there be any need for me to behave like anything more than a visitor. In fact, after further reflection, I decided that it would be best to consider myself as a sort of stranger in this modest (and suitably furnished) bedroom, to behave like a stranger, to think like a stranger, to reflect as a stranger would on the best way to live in the bedroom. My presence would be tolerated and nothing more. Was it not best to begin by adapting myself to the strict limits of the role I was supposed to play in my new environment? In truth, my role would be secondary and, in any case, only partially defined: I was to exist in the background (in this bedroom) (in which I was to always feel more or less like a stranger). A role that, in all honesty, was perfect for me. Because of not only a lack of sufficient

3

lighting, but also a distracting tendency to feel complete responsibility for my isolation, I had difficulty distinguishing the limits and contours of myself under the weak rays of my bedroom's lightbulb, suspended and swinging above my head. Something was telling me I should recognize that my situation was actually quite desirable, everything taken into account (especially when considering all the evils I'd escaped). I was free, after all, to leave the scene at any moment. I had only to imagine myself in the bedroom, solitary, undecided, a prisoner of a room I had no desire to leave, to appreciate the benefits of my present condition. I had some trouble deciding what to do with myself in my new environment; I think I had begun to forget who I'd been before finding myself in this bedroom. My memories had also lost their sharpness and precision, their brilliant luminosity, seductive but misleading. I distracted myself from time to time by reminiscing about my former life (more or less happy), experiencing in the process precisely the same sensation I get when trying to decipher the faded labels on worn-out pieces of clothing. Filling the hours, occupying myself as best as I could (and with more success than one might expect). There was no one else other than me in my imaginary bedroom, and thus no risk of compromising or confusing myself (mistaking myself for someone else). I was completely alone, at last; without worry, without concern. No one else could take my place, and nobody could dispute the role I had to play in the bedroom, in *my* bedroom.

I'd imagined that it would take a certain amount of time for me to get used to the bedroom, probably even more time than it would take to get used to an ordinary bedroom. It's not easy to take a vacation from one's habits, one's regrets, from the endless arguments and meaningless conflicts that form the foundation of a life already underway. One tries first of all to reestablish one's sanity, and so I also tried first of all to reestablish my sanity, to put my ideas into order. *There was no longer anyone waiting for me, let there be no misunderstanding.* To challenge my memory, with its unexpected, nearly blinding appearances, then learn to rid memory from my thoughts when it begins to hinder my reflections. I wasn't there by chance, or I could at least convince myself I wasn't by concentrating on the specifics of my surroundings, by pacing around the room and carefully examining it, giving each detail and each square centimeter my highest level of attention. Had I not achieved some sort of victory? Or rather: was there any reason not to use the resources of my imagination to convince myself that I'd achieved some sort of victory, had overcome numerous obstacles, had eluded the many traps I'd set for myself? Who knows, maybe everything that had made my life impossible had been my own doing. And now that I was here, by my own choosing, I needed to reason a little, to figure out how I had finally ended up here, a task that required bringing past difficulties into relation with the precise circumstances that had precipitated those difficulties, circumstances which were mostly unknown to me (at that moment) (to me who had no desire to remember the person I once was) (no desire to remember his habits, his intentions, his passions). But why did the memory attached to my own self, to my voice, to my eccentricities, have the power to give rise to such struggles within me? I now had all the time I wanted for self-interrogation, for intense reflection upon my past circumstances and, eventually, on the relationship between those circumstances and my present situation (in the bedroom). To contemplate from the very first day (and with the greatest possible urgency) how to best begin this new life, even if this contemplation gave rise to new difficulties. Finally, it would perhaps be best if I don't settle in at all, I said to myself, if I never begin to feel completely at home, if I tell myself I'm nothing but a stranger in a temporary room.

In a hotel room, I know from experience, one always ends up feeling at home and at peace. Move a piece of furniture, even just an ashtray, draw the curtains to let in some light—these gestures are simple, precise, effective: the room suddenly belongs to you, for a night or for a year. Even the sound the door makes (the door to the room), after one or two repetitions (open, close, reopen, close again), quickly becomes familiar. But I wasn't at a hotel (in a hotel room). The bedroom (my bedroom, so to speak) resisted all attempts at conciliation; it didn't want me there. I would never feel at home, I was sure of it. In a final attempt at appeasement, I resolved to vividly imagine all the reasons my stay might be opposed, being ready at all times to move out at the slightest unfavorable sign. Even if one day I came to feel completely comfortable, I still wouldn't allow myself to take any real pride in that comfort. I know that appearances can be misleading. Remain constantly vigilant, always alert, I said to myself, never let your guard down. And continue, despite everything, your exploration (exploration of the bedroom) in the hope that some truth about yourself might be revealed at any moment. What else was there for me to do? No one ever visited me, and I didn't want to be visited anyway, there was nobody I wanted to see. I was contemplating something, that much is certain, I was trying to find a precise direction for my contemplation, to fix it on a specific subject. And, indisputably, I was alone; no one, for once, could interrupt my contemplation. I needed to contemplate how to meaningfully occupy myself (to think about finding an occupation) (which itself was already an occupation, a serious undertaking). And it is in these moments of contemplation, I would say to myself, that no one can do anything to *harm you*.

There is no need to worry about other people: *they are else-where.* In my bedroom, in my new state of being, I no longer feared anything or anyone. Unknown at this address. I'd done everything necessary to ensure that no one knew I was here, shut away in this cage of a building on the eleventh floor. I'd played my part in the great chore of life (ignore them all, I told myself, pretend to be dead), I'd had my own habits and routines, the accumulated experience, the years of work. Now all I wanted was a tower at the far end of a large city, with windows looking out onto a freeway. *Among all the possible lives, you have to choose one.* Beyond, a forest; the trees rise stiffly up out of the ground, their tops make silhouettes in the distance. Cars go speeding by, and when night falls their headlights project sudden flashes into the trees. Their lights never reach the heart of the forest. The tower was silent, everything was strangely calm. I was completely and beauti-fully unknown at this address, I had no doubts about that. I'd chosen to be there, in a complete and ideal solitude ((alone in my tower) (with no one and nothing around)). Assured of being truly alone, telling myself: they'll never find me again, my tracks have been covered. (Maybe they'll even start to forget me.) *You must choose a life and anchor yourself to that life.* Those who would try to see me again (and I knew such people existed and would exist always and would continue to exist after my death and even after their own deaths (for all eternity, so to speak) (and despite my attempts to ignore their existence)), I could never object to their existence nor could

I reproach them for trying to see me (see me again), and in all honesty, it was all the same to me whether they looked for me or not, they could search for me as much as they wanted, I didn't care, I'd found ways to keep them out of my thoughts. They had no chance, and that's a fact, of finding me where I was (and where I felt so far away from everything); their existence didn't bother me at all. So I was alone (there where I was, my eyes closed, there was no one but me) in the bedroom, feeling rather sure of myself, with several foggy memories. I rarely left my bedroom, as rarely as possible in fact, and although I was the principal (and sole) occupant of this rarely left bedroom, I found that I couldn't get over the feeling that at any moment I could be scolded for my insignificance, for my lack of initiative, and that I might be asked, for these reasons (or other reasons) (even more unfair), to leave. I would have felt too weak to defend or justify my choices. It was my bedroom's responsibility to play the star-ring role (at least in my conception of an existence in a bed-room that was supposed to be my own), and I still felt no need to scrutinize my new condition: alone in my bedroom, deprived of the principal role and the responsibilities of that role. I've always thought that the character of a man (his temperament and his potential) was formed between four walls, in those several square meters one calls a bedroom and that constitute in some way his most vital space. *Among all the possible lives, you must choose a life and then anchor yourself to that life in order to be able to contemplate, serenely, all the other possibilities.* So here you are, I would say to myself (and I'd already had this thought before), you've found this bedroom and nothing can force you now to leave it. You will be able to lock yourself away and stay locked away (and isolated) as long as you want and to contemplate all the lives you haven't lived and all the lives you will never live. As long as it is humanly possible to stay locked away in a bedroom and hold on to this role, I repeated to myself. This is a good decision, it must be said. And when you do decide to do it, when you have decided to go out, when you've made this decision, you will indeed leave the bedroom, you will immediately execute your decision to leave. This, and nothing more, is your role, I said to myself, this is a good beginning. I was happy to have found this word, I was happy to have pronounced it: decision. I was fortunate to have found the right word at the right moment. At some point or another, it's important to begin something. I've always believed that. I rent this bedroom (at a modest price) and since I have lived here I haven't once considered complaining about my lot.

I woke up one morning and my sickness had disappeared; just the day before, I'd been shouting threats I saw written in red on the palm of my hand. *The next day you find that the sentences have become illegible, were erased.* Now that I'm no longer sick, I feel that I've found a room perfectly adapted to my plans (to find and develop my possibilities), this perfect sickroom where I no longer have any trace of sickness and where I have no need of anything or anyone (and above all the care of anyone). I don't need much ink to describe this bedroom (this perfect sickroom, if you like) in which for several weeks I've lived the life of a well-adjusted man (that is to say: a normal and ordinary life, the life of man whose health is no longer a concern for anybody). My health is good (restored), and as for the psychiatric services on which I depended for several months, there's no doubt that I have once again become, thanks to the care (or in spite of the care) provided by these services, capable of leading a normal life, that is to say, capable of walking through the streets should I find the desire to do so, freely and responsibly (like anyone else), and of living alone in my own bedroom (where nobody has the right to enter without my formal permission). I should mention that my recovery is (still) a mystery. *The next day, in my parents' house, I read and repeated as loudly as I could, while circling the kitchen, the name of a brand of detergent stored beneath the kitchen sink, I repeated the name until it took on a greater significance, until my brain began to experience the aural satisfaction one gets when hearing words like* firmament, absolute, depression, *until in my mind there was no difference between the brand of detergent and the word* truth. *I looked at my hand (once again). I could no longer decipher the sentence or recognize that I'd written something (there), and my hand had become completely red, frightening, hostile. Madame Violeta herself, psychic and palm reader, would have been incapable of finding any meaning in it. I had a hand without a future and I smiled weakly as I began pouring detergent into my palm. Then I made a fist and raised it as if I meant to threaten myself.*

Who am I? Nobody. This is an evasive response, of course, and I'm fully aware of its insufficiency: it's the only response that comes to mind, however (at the moment) (or rather in the moment immediately following the question); but I should be excused for my lack of imagination (which is making me clarify all this). I ask myself this question often, in any case. At different moments of my existence I've asked myself the question (who am I), and I continue to ask it today, using the same burdensome words arranged in the same unalterable order (I've written it now in my notebook, in an attempt to rid myself of the question and all of the problems that go along with it, and to observe as clearly as possible my incapacity to formulate any meaningful ideas on the subject of my hypothetical self). And these are the words

I feel an inexorable impulse to write, without any real consideration of what they mean and without any defense against the impulse that makes me put them down onto paper, as if it is best to have them written out, even if I regret them immediately after, than to have said nothing at all on the subject of myself. Nobody, in fact, is the name I've most often given myself (and that I give to myself at any particular moment (and without the slightest reflection)) in those moments when I ask myself who I am, and (in those moments) when I find no other response than: nobody (a response that I know is mostly worthless). I would like to be distinguished by some notable characteristic, some kind of physical mark that would set me apart, something of exception, but I can find nothing that would merit attention. I can find nothing remarkable about my body, although I have often searched myself and have tried, countless times, to examine myself discretely and find (discretely) something about my body that I could admire (something which could be to my advantage or disadvantage, it wouldn't matter, but which would be a source of perpetual (or at least lasting) contentment for me, insofar as I would feel, because of this feature, different from others). Despite this, my answer is still, as I said, nobody (my definitive response), or if one prefers, a person among others, a dull person whose character is without distinction (in which one sees nothing worthy of admiration or even consideration). But I don't like this response (I admit this without anger or resentment), or rather I should say that this response doesn't satisfy me. I don't mean to say that this response isn't satisfying in itself, I don't blame it for its falseness or its lack of definition (because I myself have no clear definition), but I believe that neither for me (who asks the question) nor for anyone else (to whom the question is unimportant anyway) can this response be satisfactory.

To be ugly, for example. So that everyone sees this physical (or perhaps moral) ugliness and never again forgets me (can't ever again forget me, from the moment they encounter me and notice this ugliness (be it physical or moral)). I've often thought about being ugly, about becoming ugly. Yes, I would like to be ugly (yes), distinguished by an ugliness that displays me to the world and forces me every morning to see (reflected in the mirror) both a cruelness and a festering rage. An ugliness without parallel that is unforgivably offensive to anyone who sees me. Every morning I stand before my mirror (which hangs above my sink), and every morning I spend a rather long and tedious time in front of the mirror observing my reflection. This exercise of self-scrutiny in the mirror, I should add, is both vain and exhausting, and I experience no pleasure in doing it, in standing alone and facing myself, that is to say, facing my own image: a trying (and even humiliating) exercise which causes throbbing headaches that sometimes last the entire day (and then into the night and the following day, and so on into the rest of the week), headaches that could accurately be described as without end. This, then (as I thought this morning), is my greatest desire: to be ugly and to see the world as an ugly person would, to see the world as it can only be seen (perceived) by someone truly ugly (or (if one prefers) objectively ugly, independent of his own judgment and the judgment of others), and not like any other normal person, deprived of the slightest distinction both on his body and in his character. I've always thought that somebody ugly would see the world differently, must see the world differently, from somebody beautiful (for example), and differently from anyone who isn't ugly, and I've always thought that an ugly man perceives the world infinitely better than a normal man (the world and its infinite complexities). An ugly man must be overwhelmed by fear, an immense amount of fear that he hides away in containers buried deep beneath the ground, and the world that fills him with this fear is the real and authentic world, that is to say, the worthless and miserable world (and not the false world perceived by a normal human being convinced of not being ugly, of not being offensive to either himself (in his own eyes) or to others (in the eyes of others)). Somebody ugly naturally notices all kinds of things that nobody else notices, the sight of which give him some idea of the inexhaustible misery stored at the bottom of every man's heart. This man is disillusioned by the world of beauty and lies because he possesses a persistent, depressive instinct that causes him to hate both life and his own living self. Buried under the ground, there are containers filled with fear, and the honest person knows, in the core of his being, that fear is the only authentic emotion a man is capable of feeling. And he knows also that eventually these containers will crack and explode and that the earth itself will soon overflow with everything contained in these haphazardly stored jars. The ugly man, a man who is without compassion, more immediately and more clearly than anyone else, perceives the sickly fear that contaminates the world, and for this, he suffers. He knows that the world is sick and he knows that, beyond suicide, there is no other future for those who no longer want to be a part of it (a part of the world).

I can spend a long time scrutinizing my face in the mirror, looking closely at every detail, without seeing any sign of sincerity (any sign of this kind). I am not even ugly, my face cannot be categorized as either an ugly face or a beautiful face. It is a face unworthy of categorization, if you will, the face of anybody. Mirrors can be found anywhere, hanging in every bedroom, every bathroom; it is impossible to avoid seeing myself and encountering my face, a face unworthy of categorization that poses no risk of offending anybody. Nobody's vision or judgment is at risk of being offended by this face. I've carried out this examination of my face a great number of times (by now) and my curiosity has dried up. The strict truth is established. If I saw myself in the street, I would not, I believe, stop to engage myself in conversation (I would almost certainly keep my eyes on the ground and cross to the other side of the street to avoid any interaction (supposing that this event should ever come about) (which seems to me quite impossible) (to speak truthfully)). If I think of Cathie, for example, and if I imagine meeting her in the street, I recognize immediately that this is something that could never happen, because I know that my face means nothing to her, that she would not recognize me and the encounter would not take place, or rather (I should say) the encounter is impossible and doomed to failure, made impossible by the simple fact that she passes by without seeing me, that she is incapable of seeing me. For Cathie and for anybody else, I'm nothing but a face among others, I am only a shadow for her now; I imagine Cathie coming down the street, and I imagine myself in the same street, walking in her direction, I imagine that I am on my way to meet Cathie and that I force myself to raise my eyes towards her and look directly into her face. I recognize her face, I recognize her, Cathie, but because of the way she's dressed, I have the impression that her face has changed, and yet I recognize her all the same, at the very last moment, as I pass by and meet her eyes with mine. But she sees nothing, she notices neither my face nor the disappointment on it, she notices nothing. At the hospital Cathie never said that I was ugly, she never said anything like that, in fact, she never said anything about me, although I'd done everything I could to make myself a nuisance (in her eyes), to inspire a kind of disgust in her by flaunting my moral degradation before her eyes. I tried everything I could think of to make her love me, I wanted her to love me for my degradation, which I forced upon myself in the hope that it might give me some chance to exist in her eyes, an existence defined by cruelness, by me being cruel. She never told me this (that I was ugly or contemptible), and she never, I believe, gave me the slightest reproach (not even a hint of one), and because of this I always suffered to some degree, being convinced that she wanted to (at least a little bit) and never did, out of fear that it might hurt my feelings or make me violent, which was in my eyes the strongest possible proof she could give me of her indifference.

Finally one evening, it must be nine o'clock, I can no longer stand being shut away in my bedroom, and so I start off down the stairwell. I've been shut away in my bedroom for too long and my solitude has become intolerable. I must find a telephone; this, in fact, is why I've left my bedroom. I go down the stairs, the sound of my feet resonates off the steps, it's a sound that cannot be muffled. Two floors below mine, I stop, I knock two quick times on the first door I find (with no response), then on a second door just across the hallway, again two quick times, with almost no space between the knocks. I'm going to find a telephone, I'll knock all night if I have to, I say to myself while waiting for someone to open, and I don't know why I'm so sure that I'm knocking on the right door, that the telephone I'm searching for is behind this specific door, but I still have to be patient, to wait for someone to open. I don't know that Sauvage is behind this door, I don't know that he's seated this evening as he is every other evening in his armchair, to tell the truth I'm not thinking about anything besides the telephone that I'll find inside, and in any case I'm prepared to knock on all the doors in the building to find what I want. I have the number on a piece of paper, I have the ten digits in my possession. I don't know where Cathie is, I don't know what she's doing, my mind's awareness is currently reduced to memorizing these ten simple digits by heart. There's nothing left to do now but dial this number (these ten digits): I know that she'll answer, she must answer, how could she do anything else, I think, sure of myself and not feeling the slightest doubt, no matter where she is, I say to myself, she'll pick up her phone and I will hear her voice, and I'll have accomplished some piece of a greater goal when I hear that voice. These ideas are based on nothing, but now that I have thought them, I don't want to lose them, I no longer have any uncertainty about myself: I have to see her again, and I have a number in my hand which is irrefutable proof that she's out there, that she might be waiting, and I don't know anymore what to do with this piece of paper, with her writing on it, now that I've had these ideas, this number written by Cathie's hand, I stare at it and I begin feeling dizzy. I'd asked her to write something, whatever she wanted, I'd said, playing the gentleman, and she wrote down her phone number on the casually offered piece of paper; but then I'd forgotten about the paper's existence. I left the hospital (before Cathie left the hospital), I was finally out, but I never knew if she'd gotten out, if she'd left the hospital, had forgotten the hospital and learned to live outside of it, but then I rediscovered her number, proof that I hadn't imagined her and that Cathie had actually existed and that I'd known her (at the hospital). The number was in my hand, I knew it by heart, but still I didn't want to lose it, I didn't want to forget about it a second time. I remember Cathie, my memory of her is clear: it's Cathie that I knew at the hospital, I tell myself, and I can no longer stop thinking about her, for two hours now I've thought about nothing but her, I don't think I'll be able to live much longer if I don't see her, and I ask myself all kinds of questions on the subject of Cathie, about the life she's leading, and I can't explain to myself why I haven't already begun looking for her (and why I've spent so much time locked in my bedroom). The day I left the hospital, I swore to myself I would never try to find her, but that same day, just before leaving, I can't say why, maybe for the beauty of the gesture and so I could remind myself of its beauty later, I ask her *to write me something* on the piece of paper, so she takes the paper and writes down the number I have in my hand today. Cathie, I foolishly promised myself while folding my fingers over the piece of paper, I'll never try to see you again, I'll remember your hand, your final gesture, such a beautiful gesture, and the paper that passed from my hand into yours, a tiny white piece of paper, as fragile as a sail approaching an ominous horizon, and on which you carefully put down your number, but that will be the end of the story, I said to myself again, even more foolishly than before. And this evening, because of this piece of paper, which is not only a memento of the past but the past itself, my old life has come hurtling back and I tell myself that this paper is a witness to a time not yet over, this paper says that I knew her and that I loved her up until my final day at the hospital and that I love her still. I'm in my bedroom, I am shut away in my bedroom, *I have to see her again* (I say to myself, shut away in my bedroom). As soon as I recognized her handwriting, I could see her smile again, a smile that in my mind now seems like the strangest thing a face can do, a miracle if you like, this smile that I see somewhere in front of me and which seems to be the cause of sudden and inexplicable phenomena, the reason why I can't remain one more second in my bedroom, which has suddenly become as suffocating and depressing as a jail cell, and why I've finally deserted it. And while watching her smile at me again, because it's her smile I now see on the paper

and the smile is meant for no one but me, I think I can hear
the cracking of ice (unless it's the softer noise of something
ripping) (of a piece of fabric being ripped apart). And I think
of her smile, suddenly shining upon and warming everything
inside me that has become a prisoner of the cold. This smile
that carried me away to the farthest ends of the earth, to the
seas of ice and the ice-breaking ships whose duty it is to create
the navigable routes in the Arctic Circle. The world's most
powerful engines propel these ships through the icy seas, the
ships that open up paths for all the other boats. And I find
myself again in the stairwell, without really considering what
I'm doing, I run down the steps as quickly as I can and stop
two floors below, I begin knocking on doors, all while telling
myself: this might be the wrong door, but nothing can stop
me from knocking on it. And her smile is still in front of me,
and with the image of the ships being propelled for thousands
of miles by impossibly powerful motors, through the cold,
through the unadulterated silence and solitude of the Arctic
night, her smile breaks through the ice that has been building
up inside me since the beginning of winter.

I'd done everything I possibly could to stop thinking about
Cathie, I'd done everything I could to forget her, and yet now
I'd been unable to get her out of my thoughts for two full
hours. She was here again, smiling at me through the window
of my memory. For two hours I couldn't stop thinking about
her, and while the piece of paper went on trembling in my
hand I repeated over and over to myself (without ever taking
my eyes off the paper), I cannot see Cathie again, she cannot
come back into my life, and I repeated these words in an
attempt to convince myself that I wouldn't break the promise
I'd made to myself and try to see her again, because to see

Cathie again, I repeated to myself, would be to let in the sadness of the past. I had to think above all of protecting myself from the past, from the people of the past, and especially from Cathie (whom I'd loved) (as I'd never loved anyone before), this is why I said and repeated to myself that I would do nothing to see her, and I repeated it over and over in the hope that the paper held between my fingers would cease to exist or suddenly burst into flames (in my hand, which was holding it), but the paper ignored my wishes (while my hand itself had done nothing to get rid of it), I'd stared at it for several long minutes while repeating that I shouldn't try to find Cathie, but it didn't disappear, it was still in my hand, intact, displaying the completely legible, unharmed number. I'd chased Cathie from my thoughts, and at the same time I'd erased the memory of my previous life. My life was no longer the same (life), it was another life, a life to be lived, that I was going to begin (to live) far away from the memory of any other life. My life had taken a new direction, my life without Cathie had begun, I'd even marked down the date of this change somewhere (I'm sure I wrote it down somewhere), but by finding this piece of paper again I realized that Cathie had really never left my thoughts. My life was meant to take a decisive turn, that's why I was in this bedroom, to begin a new life and to savor every detail of that new life, but at each moment Cathie had been in my thoughts, I'd never actually stopped thinking about her, and I'd only needed to find the piece of paper to realize it. I rediscovered it, the piece of paper, slipped into a novel by Hamsun, on page 104; I'd wanted to reread Hamsun (one passage in particular), so I opened *Hunger* to page 104, and it wasn't what Hamsun had written on page 104 that caught my attention but the telephone number on the piece of paper. I have the Norwegian writer's novel in my hand, I found it somewhere among my things, and I realize that Cathie hasn't ceased to exist, Cathie is still alive, the numbers in her handwriting tell me this, I haven't forgotten her, she's left me a sign in Hamsun's book, on page 104: I must see her again. This entire time she'd taken another form, changed her essence, but I'd understood nothing about her transformation, she was no longer in my thoughts and I'd forgotten about the telephone number, hidden, or at least set aside, in Hamsun's novel. I'd understood nothing. Cathie hadn't left me, and I hadn't left Cathie, she wasn't far from me, hidden in Hamsun's novel, nor was I far from her, at any moment I could have found her by opening Hamsun's novel. It would have been impossible to forget her or chase her from my thoughts, I told myself as I closed the book, because during the entire time I thought I'd forgotten her, she was still in Hamsun's book, a book I know by heart.

And so I found myself before this door, two floors down, and to distract myself while waiting for a response, to stop the obnoxious countdown in my head, I tried to make out the name on Sauvage's doorbell, written in pencil and almost illegible, and I considered erasing the name and replacing it with another one, completely made-up, imagining the supernatural consequences that might result from the act, the irreversible metamorphosis of the man once named Sauvage, forced from then on to go about his apartment with the movements and voice of somebody else, attacked perhaps by sudden spasms that would gradually distort his true face, condemned from then on to present to others the mannerisms and gestures of another man, all while being completely incapable of denouncing the imposture. Maybe there was no one there, or maybe, if there was someone behind the door, he (named Sauvage) wouldn't bother responding, perhaps he was even incapable of responding, I thought, because by changing his name in my imagination, I'd destroyed his substance and being. No matter who answered, I said to myself then, I would never be able to confirm whether or not I'd altered this man's life, and the thought that I could never be sure of the true identity of the unresponsive person behind the door severely upset me. But someone had finally responded, in a polite voice with a touch of fear in it, a voice that struck me immediately as strange and made me think of a frightened animal trembling at the back of its cage. I pushed open the door, entered the apartment, and after crossing a short hallway, encouraged by a voice, inhuman and yet familiar, saying, Come in, come in, I found myself in a dark room filled with books, and I could make out the silhouette of a heavy man sitting with his back to me. Come in, he repeated as if for himself and without moving from his armchair, and though I didn't know why, I understood he had no intention of switching on a light or making me feel at ease. I have to make an urgent phone call, I heard myself say in a voice that seemed somehow altered, addressing the unknown man, or, rather, addressing his back, whose outline I could now make out better (now that my eyes had adjusted to the dark) in the backlight coming in through the blue and black parallelogram of his window. I saw that he was seated at a desk, busy either reading or writing, and I assumed that he probably hadn't moved from his place for hours, that he'd no doubt been working a long time without any rest at his far too narrow desk, surrounded by piles of books and folders. Something told me that he suffered from an enormous fatigue, a fatigue as immense and ancient as the earth itself. He won't even turn to look at me, I thought to myself, feeling more and more unwelcome as the seconds passed by without a response. Go ahead, he said at last, after a deathlike silence, and pointed with his finger to a telephone resting on the floor. And so it was in this unsettling darkness that I mechanically dialed the number I'd read and reread thousands of times.

It wasn't Cathie's voice, the nocturnal voice that answered and told me I must have the wrong number, and while I was willing to admit to the possibility of a mistake, I was still far from ready to accept that Cathie might have been trying to mislead me. I might have been mistaken, maybe I'd called on the wrong day or at the wrong time, but I could call again at any moment, I said, whenever Cathie wanted me to, several times in a row if it's necessary, I might have been mistaken, it's possible, but the error was human, reparable, so easy to set straight. I repeated that I wanted to talk to Cathie, she'd given me this number two months ago, ten complete digits, a clear message, perfectly legible, unaffected by the crease in the paper, I have to speak to her now, it is absolutely necessary that I know where she is, where I can find her, it's extremely important for me, I added, to know what has become of her. You have the wrong number, the voice repeated impatiently. There's no Cathie here, are you sure that it's Cathie you want to speak to and not someone else? The voice sounds strangely different than it did a moment ago. I begin to feel uncertain about Cathie's name and about my own intentions, so easily crushed by this setback; I start searching through my memory as quickly as I can, considering that maybe Cathie lied to me, that she gave me a random number to get rid of me, an unwanted nuisance in her life, maybe it was the number of an asylum, or a home for young women handicapped by blindness, and beginning on this evening, and continuing through the evenings to come, I would feel a growing desperation in the face of my undeniable powerlessness to contact her. It was always a woman that answered, though never the same one twice, and night after night I would have the impression that

I was calling for the first time, that I had to reestablish who I was, pick up the conversation from the very beginning, a conversation interrupted the day before because of fatigue, incomprehension, or indifference, but one that I had to restart every day in order to explain that Cathie had to be close by, that only a small effort was required to remember who she was and to determine where she could be. I would ask for Cathie, to speak to Cathie, and the voice (every night a different voice, or, as was my impression, the same voice but subtly modified, a single voice that had the ability to change from one day to the next, unless the variations in tone were simply a reflection of the daily differences in the air, the circumstances, etc.) would ask back: What is it that you really want? And all the impatience that had been building up inside me would suddenly come to a head, and I'd have to fight back a suspicion that she was under orders to mislead me. I would hang up without another word and swallow my frustration and shame, desperately hoping that the next day Cathie would finally answer, laughing and having forgotten everything, the past, my cruelty, the distance that had grown between us: I'm here because you've proven yourself to be patient, she would say, adding that we would never again be apart, but that I still had to wait a little longer, she still needed some time before she could see me, not a lot of time, we'll be together soon, she would whisper, tomorrow or the day after, I'll be entirely yours. My head would then begin filling with an image of Cathie sitting on my knees, an image I'd carefully stored within the depths of my mind for fear of losing it. And, I would think, was it not also the right moment to remember the many times I made her cry and to carefully recreate and then memorize, for future reference, her eyes, her breasts, her tears?

But on that first evening, Sauvage, perhaps sensing my frustration, didn't make the slightest allusion to what had happened on the phone, and I soon forgot what had first brought me into his small apartment. I could see his silhouette better now that my eyes had adjusted, though it was still impossible to make out his face: he seemed to be kilometers away, taking cold refuge in the silence and darkness of his room. Without turning to face me, he made a brief motion with his hand, the significance of which I immediately understood, and, at his invitation, I turned on the overhead light and seated myself in a folding chair that had been leaning against a wall. A forty-watt lightbulb hanging in the exact center of the ceiling lit up and filled the room with a dirty-white light. My eyes instinctively made a quick examination of the room: books were strewn everywhere, on the shelves, on the floor, and I experienced a feeling of suffocation in the tight, confined space, where any movement seemed like it would be a pointless waste of energy. A row of Russian dolls was carefully arranged along the windowsill, creating a stark effect of contrast with the room's other objects. I looked successively from doll to doll, as if each one of them might contain some kind of secret: they all shared the same features, the same blond locks falling from the temples, the same prominent red cheekbones, the same childish, or perhaps ironic, smile. I examined them carefully, trying to recreate the story of their exile, until my attention was distracted by a scraping noise coming from the feet of Sauvage's armchair. It happened incredibly fast and without any visible effort; with a speed that could be called miraculous, Sauvage had deftly maneuvered his armchair across the room. He was now less than one meter away from me, yet I hadn't seen him move at all. Was I afraid to face his judgment, feeling undisguised and like I had no way of concealing my thoughts? I waited

a moment and then turned towards him. My first thought
upon seeing him up close was that I wouldn't have been
able to guess his age. His almost otherworldly mouth, like
something out of a dream or the result of a mutation, was
formed into a curious pout, while the rest of his face seemed
to be beyond his control. I blamed the electric light, falling
weakly over our heads, for the discomfort I was feeling, and
I forced a smile to hide my anxiety. He seemed inhuman,
unapproachable, as calm as a sleeping fortress under a sun
of chalk, but, nevertheless, I couldn't push away a fear that
he might suddenly explode into violence. Because under the
weak, artificial glow of the lightbulb, Sauvage's body belied
an insidious and inexorable force. I can still remember the
feeling of passivity and powerlessness I experienced before
this man who seemed to be fused to his chair, not as a prisoner or dependent, but as the master of an object that had
fallen under his influence. I can see myself again on that
evening, facing his body, which seemed as vast and immobile
as an empire. I'm frozen, stuck in my chair with no means of
escape or resistance, incapable of taking the slightest initiative
or making any movement in the yellow room, and I consider Sauvage's strange and enormous silhouette and find that
while I'm being observed so tranquilly by Sauvage, so calmly
and even with a trace of benign curiosity, I cannot take control of my thoughts. Enthroned upon his chair, he looks at
me as an etymologist might look at an insect; I feel like he
can see my thoughts, can read me as easily as he would one
of his books; I'm somewhat embarrassed, I notice a glimmer
of interest in his expression, of satisfaction or irony (I'm not
certain which), and at the same time I'm persuaded that the
reasons for his amused attention are both unknowable and
impenetrable; I cannot seize the meaning of his stare, which
seems to originate from some cruel and devastated region and
which even I, in the same room, cannot reach. My thoughts
are defenseless, I fear they will soon crumble into dust or

(worse) be annexed by those of my neighbor, and I suddenly have a desire to exert myself, to understand and pierce the enigma of the body, of its flesh, I am filled with a lust and desire to know, *to pass to the other side*, to reach that point of fusion inaccessible to both examination and reason.

Finally, after making a slight defensive movement, caused perhaps by a deep regret at allowing a stranger a glimpse of his soul, he opens his mouth and begins to speak, staring at me intensely, as if he were looking through a magnifying glass. I am a translator (he says slowly) (while his eyes go on scrutinizing, deciphering, examining), and I immediately feel the immeasurable weight and depth contained in these words: *I am a translator*, this was his life, his vocation and his prison (right here in this very place) in the small, dimly lit room that he must have almost never left, due to an inability to feel at ease anywhere else. For several months, in fact, he's been occupied with the translation of a scientific work, the scope of which goes beyond the imagination of a simple mortal (which I am in his eyes) (and also in my own eyes). An immense and, in some ways, frightening task, which would have already killed him if he hadn't found a way, during the intervals between his arduous and taxing work, to calm himself by listening to records (records of classical music) (recognizable by their familiar yellow label: Deutsche Grammophon). Music and translation being twin sisters, he claims, that destiny has condemned to live eternally together. Poor imitation of a couple, I think, imagining the dreary and toilsome life of the two inseparable sisters who, under a guise of attachment and affection, go about their life under the same roof, sleeping in the same bed, sharing the same hobbies, eating a tasteless meal at the same time and same table every night, with no chance of ever being able to stop seeing, and thus hating, one another. It is *The Dictionary of Rare and Incurable Illnesses* that fills up his days and deprives him of any hobbies or diversions. Illness begins with a name, and he spells out this name in his mind, isolating the syllables to better immerse himself in them, lending an ear to the music hidden in their combinations. Though they are sometimes listed under their Latin name, more often an incurable illness is named after the researcher who discovered it: Churg and Strauss, Wegener, Behçet, Takayasu; you can't forget the forbidding, off-putting tonality of these names, which resonate like promises of exile. Sauvage explains degenerative illness to me; he can say everything with a precision that I envy. He speaks of an unannounced stranger from a far-off place who decides one day to make his home in the body of a man or a woman. The host doesn't understand why the stranger has decided to stop here in his body, a body which is incapable of understanding the guest's language and soon finds itself struggling to breathe and walk, to make the most basic movements, to even recognize its own voice. The disease has taken hold, its evolution has become unstoppable and its symptoms cannot be ameliorated: it deforms the body and pushes its human host towards a most cruel and programmed death. The man who once had control over his life, who was attached to his own body, to his habits, his friends, his thoughts, now becomes a stranger to himself (in his own body). For every illness that he names (with obvious delight), Sauvage can recite by heart a complete list of corresponding symptoms (as well as the prognosis and probable course of treatment). The most obscure and enigmatic diseases—a spectrum that includes everything from degenerative bone disease to mitral stenosis—hide no secrets from this man who translates into an irreproachable French a description of their symptoms, of their progress and complications, which can range from blindness to loss of balance to difficulties recognizing loved

ones; after solemnly picking up a page from the pile on his
desk, he reads me extracts from his translation-in-progress,
and, with a rapidity that horrifies me, I become familiar with
histiocytosis X, allergic granulomatosis, and giant congenital
nevus. When he finishes reading, he glances quickly in my
direction, as if to measure my degree of discomfort. He isn't
a doctor, he assures me when he's caught his breath, although
he has always felt drawn towards disease and has even entered
into a sort of complicity with disease, he says. A doctor, in
some sense, is an author, a creator in the realm of medicine.
While Sauvage, according to himself, belongs to an inferior
circle, whose members dwell in unsurprising anonymity and
can expect neither recognition nor praise for what they do. So
many times, says Sauvage, he's felt the hopeless insufficiency
of language, so many times he's described the terrible illness
that lies smoldering behind each definition. Whether or not
language is a bastardization of thought, he says, he is its first
witness, the pure witness. All doctors are naturally taciturn,
this is an undeniable fact that he's observed many times, and
if he himself had become a doctor, there is no doubt that he
would also have surrounded himself with the most profound
silence; but he's also forced to acknowledge an unexpected
consequence of the translator's responsibility, and the inher-
ent difficulty and despair that go along with it: he is more
qualified than anyone else to speak about disease. Sauvage
watches me with an intense curiosity, in which I can discern
the reason for my fear. His words begin to pour out faster,
and my fascination with him increases. All of the science contained in his dictionaries: Sauvage claims to have absorbed
it all. Swallowed and digested, all of the science contained
within them (he says), yes, I've learned everything that's written in those dictionaries, he repeats while motioning with
an imperceptible movement of his head to the two rows of
volumes arranged behind him. I'm unsure how to respond, so
I sit motionless before him, as if paralyzed, and then briefly

turn my head to look at the dictionaries. A vague sensation of annoyance or confusion has begun to take hold of me and my thoughts feel like they've grown numb, turning over and over on themselves as if in a state of madness or in a dream, searching to recapture their equilibrium. Since he's begun speaking to me, only his mouth seems to have moved, while his tiny head, resting upon his overgrown shoulders, has appeared motionless; but the rest of his face, I now notice, is also very animated, his expressions rapidly changing and contradicting each other (in his overactive face that seems hypersensitive to the climactic variations in the room). And here, says Sauvage, is where all the difficulty resides: during the time it takes to fully understand a disease, to discover its limits and map its symptoms, life invents ten new ones, more subtle and more cunning than any of their predecessors, and medicine is pushed backwards into a deeper state of ignorance. Every day that goes by, I think to myself while looking at Sauvage, another page is added to the dictionary, every day our bodies create new pages, and Sauvage must devote himself to the translation of these pages, written in the obscure language of life.

I hadn't moved from where I was, daring neither to interrupt nor make the slightest sound, wondering how I would ever manage to leave the dark and damp apartment without offending this man, whom I no longer saw as a real person but as a melancholic, subterranean power under whose influence I'd now fallen. Overcome by anxiety while facing Sauvage, I wondered if I myself might sooner or later end up as absorbed, digested, and assimilated by him, and although it was impossible for me to ignore his subtle, magnetic power, I was also growing aware of a potentially extraordinary force with an existence independent of the physical power of his enormous body, lodged in the armchair, and which derived from the invisible and secret force of all the thoughts enveloped and concealed by his mass. Sauvage's mind, I thought to myself, most of the time and maybe at every moment of his existence, must be preoccupied by his body, the inertia and enormity of which must represent for him not only an obstacle but a kind of dead weight, a dead weight relentlessly and fatally dragging each one of his thoughts to the same inescapable place. Since he'd begun speaking in his excessively humble and polite voice (not unlike that of a young girl or a devout churchgoer, I thought while listening to the cyclical, harmonious music of its modulations), I couldn't stop thinking of all the disabilities that can transform a man into an impotent creature condemned to physical and moral solitude, and I played over and over in my mind all of the basic movements (seeing a mental photo gallery of everyday movements whose minute mechanisms I'd memorized over the years) that a disabled person cannot perform, the movements required to stand up, to walk, to accomplish the simplest and most necessary tasks, even the movements required to see beyond your stomach to your own organ during urination. A prisoner of his own body, forced to think constantly (and obsessively) (without respite) about his imprisonment, never able to forget it or put it into the background of his mind; I said to myself that Sauvage must experience the suffering of a martyr, condemned by his own body to continuous and unrelenting pain, not only because he must inhabit his body (we are all condemned to inhabit a body), but because he must inhabit his in the most humiliating way conceivable. And yet, I sensed, he hadn't had his final word, this man who had given up on movement and seemed so close to those beings who'd been disqualified from life, I had no doubt that he'd placed his power elsewhere, a power not of physical, brute force, but of some other nature, a power beyond both knowledge and science that was invisible to the shocked spectator I'd suddenly become. That evening, as he spoke to me for the first time about his translation, my thoughts could not stop revolving around this one astonishing and depressing subject: all the things a body cannot do, or is condemned to no longer be capable of doing, because a mutation in its flesh has so thoroughly confiscated its powers that, one after another, all of the body's functions are extinguished and removed, until even the desire for movement has been proudly conquered. Sauvage's flesh had perhaps reached a kind of perfection or greatness, I'd said to myself, and I felt unworthy of understanding and incapable of imagining what kind of happy life might have been hiding in the layers of clothing covering his body (he wore several layers of clothing to protect himself from the cold and dampness of his bedroom, giving him the appearance sometimes of a tramp, sometimes of a man caught in an eternal process of healing).

I began to visit Sauvage regularly, listening to him talk about his translation work late into the night. I would listen to him with a kind of astonished fervor, in the same way that a crowd might listen, moving briskly from feelings of approval to feelings of outrage, carried away by the force of the group while completely deprived of my own individual judgment and free will. I didn't attach much importance to the meaning of his words, letting myself instead simply be filled with the sound of his voice and the soft, benevolent fatigue that it made me feel. I would listen until his words suddenly became nothing more than simple sounds deprived of meaning, a little bit unnerving, floating like notes on an indecipherable score. He would never move from his place, with his back always turned to the window. Immobile, speaking in his breathless manner while describing the shortcomings of language, as he often did when explaining the hopelessness of the translator. It takes some getting used to, I thought more than once of his misplaced voice, so poorly paired with his body, as if it'd been stolen from someone else. I would eventually come to be convinced that a secret host had taken residence inside Sauvage's body, nailing him to his chair and forbidding him to move, condemning Sauvage to reduce his movements to the smallest possible number. This host, I would think, was starved for darkness and food, for attention and tenderness; and I would imagine the spindly orphan who'd taken root in Sauvage's body, demanding to be heated and pampered and treated like a king, demanding from Sauvage a complete and unmerciful sacrifice, depriving him of his faith, his habits, even his breathing. The orphan had been gnawing away at Sauvage's body for months, maybe for years, the little tyrant had made his home inside Sauvage's body, and now he would never leave it. And yet: Sauvage found no reason to complain; on the contrary, he seemed happy, satisfied, as astonishing as that might sound. Does Sauvage, I asked myself as I went back up the stairs to my bedroom, have the memory of another body, does he at least remember the energetic, playful child he'd once been, capable of walking and running? And I asked myself while undressing what would make me happy, I who had *chosen* to change my life and fall out of existence. You only have to close your eyes to know that you are truly alone in a black and infinite nothingness, I said to myself, once I'd found myself back in bed. I fell asleep almost immediately, and the next morning I realized, while searching through my pockets, that I had lost Cathie's number.

From time to time, we would listen to a record (often the

same record) (a Deutsche Grammophon edition). I remember the importance of music (from Sauvage's point of view) and Sauvage's well thought-out opinions (on music) (and more particularly on the therapeutic function (of music)). Sauvage tells me one evening, and I remember exactly what he said that day, probably because he enunciates each word as if he were reading it off an imaginary score: It has been repeatedly demonstrated that doctors love music more than any other art. All the greatest music lovers are doctors, and one in two doctors plays the violin or piano, Sauvage tells me, adding that there exists a secret affinity between the art of medicine and the art of music. The same impulse, he says, drives both music and medicine. All the best opera singers and musicians come from families of doctors. And the houses of doctors are houses of music, houses filled with instruments and in which music can be heard from morning until evening, on every floor of a doctor's house there's a piano or a cello and any number of other musical instruments; and I suddenly picture a doctor's daughter, getting ready to play a score she'd begun the previous day, and am overcome by a desire to be with her, in that same room. When a virtuoso appears, he continues, you can say with absolute certainty that he has come from a family of doctors. Then he falls silent. Sauvage says nothing for a long moment, and I tell myself that the silence is a response to his musical desires. He makes a small movement and I understand that he wants me to play a record. And I know which one to put on. With the sound of the first notes, we float off; our conversation is finished. The *lamento* rises, a wave of dark notes builds up, grows in power and readies itself to crash over our souls; Sauvage and I say nothing as the first dark wave rises above our heads; the slow group of violins that passes above us is like the dark, slick hull of a submarine. I watch it go by, and, like every other time we've listened to it, Górecki's symphony has a terrible and depressing effect on me, and I wonder if the composer of this somber symphony also came from a family of doctors.

Cathie often reproached me for being cruel (at the hospital). You are like the others, not better, not worse, you are cruel and nothing more, she would say (she would summarize) while watching me and smiling (and I would smile in return). I would make fun of her first name, which I found ridiculous and ugly, I would tell her over and over that she should change it, insisting that she would feel infinitely better once she'd abolished her idiotic name from her life; I would offer to find her another name (another first name) and I would promise her that this name (chosen by me) would be for her a fresh beginning, a fresh spring rain in which she could bathe and rejoice at every moment of her existence (or at least each time I shouted out the name, from the other end of the hallway, for the pleasure of her ears). How could the people who were your parents burden you with such a ridiculous name? And how have you managed to live through all these lost years, ruined by your name? Why are you surprised that you hate them so much, forced as you are to despise every square centimeter of your body, disfigured as it is by all the bitterness and violence and fear contained in your name? I loved to humiliate her and I would often recite female names to her taken at random from the phone book. You are cruel, she would simply say (as softly as she could) without a trace of cruelty, and I knew that she was sincere and absolutely devoid (or incapable) of cruelness, she didn't even try to hide from my cruelness or anger, while I went on searching for new ways to be cruel (ways to be cruel in her presence). At the hospital, I discovered that I could be cruel, and so I decided to be cruel, discovering in my cruelty the possibility of advancing in a precise direction (while sheltering myself from the judgment of others), and every time I was in Cathie's presence cruel words would form in my mouth and I would be incapable of holding them back. I was full of harsh and violent words, of phrases as cutting as the sharpened blade of a butcher's knife. I was in the hospital (and Cathie was in the same hospital), and I'd discovered the best way to get myself out from that hole where I'd been shut away. My anger and solitude had given rise to my cruelty, and by manipulating this cruelty (my instrument of cruelty) I would get myself out of there (out of that repugnant hole where my illness had led me), I knew it, I would get out, whether it was through baseness or calculation (or by any other path opened by my cruelty). I would deceive illness (my illness) using cruelty, I would overcome my illness with my persistent cruelty, by hurling cruelty from all sides and in all directions I would triumph over my illness (and the entire medical world). I was excited, and I announced my thoughts in a screeching, high-pitched voice, so that each of my words would reach their target (which was Cathie), my words were aimed for the beating heart hidden under her green nightgown (through which her naked legs could be seen), because when speaking of my illness, I was not addressing it (the illness) but Cathie (who was also sick and who I also promised to get out of there (out of that hole) (which had become our magic circle)). I had to concentrate, or rather I couldn't let myself be distracted by the sight of Cathie's defenseless young legs, on forming these words (my cruel words), so that each of my words corresponded with the cruel thought that had preceded it (so that I could find a way out) (out of the medical world). She was in front of me in her nightgown, and under the nightgown, my god, I could see blood, blood flowing through her veins, through her arteries, all the blood that was making her young heart beat. Her face was smiling, shining, and although she was not exactly beautiful (Cathie, in my memory, is ugly (or simply plain)), I loved her madly (as one says), or if you prefer, I loved her as only someone convinced of his own worthlessness can (madly) love someone he knows infinitely exceeds him (a being in whose presence he experiences a kind of self-annihilation). I loved her for her unlimited kindness or perhaps for another reason entirely, maybe because she was wearing a pale green nightgown which made her seem uglier and, in my eyes, more vulnerable (and also more beautiful in a certain way that I can't describe: an indescribable beauty (in my eyes) (which were the only ones to see it) (in the hospital)). I might have seen Cathie again sometime later outside the hospital, but I've imagined the scene so many times, in its complex and inexplicable circumstances, that I don't think I'll ever be sure if it really happened; whatever the case may be, however, I have no memory of ever experiencing again the love I'd once felt for her (which has become as imaginary as the improbable circumstances of a second encounter), or of her reproaching me for my cruelness, no doubt because I wouldn't have given her any reason to do so outside of the hospital, incapable as I now was of being cruel and demonstrating in any way my cruelty. It had suddenly become impossible for me (once out of the hospital) to demonstrate my cruelty, and as soon as I'd realized this I found that I felt disarmed, and I recognized this absence as a defeat and, more so, as an obstacle. Whatever the case may be, I had great difficulty recognizing Cathie (she'd never consented to a name change), who was no longer dressed in her delicate nightgown but was now wearing a scarlet jacket, and she certainly experienced the same difficulty in recognizing me, and all at once, we both seemed to experience an immense disappointment in realizing that we'd become strangers to each other, as if the memory of that bygone time when we spent most of the day in a nightgown (her) and pajamas (me) now left us completely cold. In the hospital, we were hardly inclined to pay much attention to our attire or, more generally, to our appearance, occupied as we were with our illnesses and the constant attention they demanded from us, encouraged throughout our hospital stay to focus our thoughts exclusively on our illnesses and, more specifically, on the quickest way to cure ourselves. At the hospital (and in no other place), I'd learned in some sense how to think, that is to say, to direct and master my thoughts, that is, to purposefully concentrate my thoughts on the goal of getting out. My mind, as long as I was at the hospital, had become, due to training and application, a kind of complex radar governing my every movement and action, and thanks to this radar my words always knew how to find their way to Cathie (with her young heart beating beneath her pale-green nightgown), but as soon as I found myself outside of the hospital, I found that my radar had been damaged and I had no idea how to repair it. And at the moment when I thought I saw Cathie in the street, I recognized my defeat in my silence and I understood that I'd lost (along with Cathie) the ability that had once saved my life.

But there you have it: she never felt threatened by me, never showed any sign of concern (or even annoyance), she was in no way afraid of me, it was as if she'd immediately accepted my presence in the translucent sphere that protected her from the aggressions of the outside world. And why me, I thought incredulously, I who had lost all my confidence, why had I been able to cross this border? I now saw the world as divided in two by a giant black line filled with landmines and barbed wire, demarcating Cathie's side of the world (heaven) from the other, a hell of treachery and lies that belonged to every-one and everything that, voluntarily or not, was threatening her life. A world impossible to reconcile or reunite. Would the silent expeditions I'd undertaken to get close to her come across as awkward attempts at flirting? *I have to believe that you didn't fear me, it seemed to me from the first moment I spoke to you that I could inspire trust in someone like you. It is certainly strange, however, that I didn't once consider that I might have made you uncomfortable. Because of our age difference, for example. This is something very difficult to explain, something that I will likely never be able to explain to myself.* Blond hair cut like Joan of Arc (although I'm aware this comparison implies something warrior-like that Cathie doesn't possess to any degree) and extremely bright, as if it'd been bleached with peroxide. As soon as I found myself close enough to begin a conversation, I began to speak openly with her, though still with many precautions, and it was immediately apparent that she couldn't hear me or even see that I was addressing her, so much did my behavior go against the expected manner of engaging in a dialogue. I'm still amazed today, yes, I am amazed that she didn't run away from me at the first chance she got. But then I understood nothing about Cathie, I often felt like I was drowning in the blue transparency of her eyes without understanding how she could stand the sight of my face or the proximity of my body, both of which were under constant assault by my unstable mind. How to explain the fact that misery could never triumph over her soft smile? That her smile, despite being full of her misery, was never miserable?

And now that I'm healthy again, something I'm sure of because I'm not in the hospital, my health has also begun to seem like a kind of defeat (and also like a good example of the futility of fighting for what you think you want). Once again,

I find myself outside of the hospital (outside of the hospital walls), outside of hospital life and all the preoccupations of hospital life, I am free again, but I also understand that I'm not completely cured. I'm in the street, I'm not in a theater or on a stage: I'm most certainly in the street, this doesn't feel like a dream. I have no war to wage now that I'm in this real-life street, which I can easily describe if I make an effort: there are cobblestones, trees, roofs, antennas, curtains, parked cars and cars in motion, power lines, cigarette butts, birds, etc. I don't have to behave out of character today, I don't need my cruelness. My cruelness, to put it another way, no longer exists. I've crossed to the other side: I'm past the gate, my permission to leave is in my pocket, I can now celebrate having crossed to the other side. I'm wearing a brand-new pair of shoes, I'm a new man, somebody appropriately and nicely dressed who strolls through the streets without a goal, without a destination (and why would anyone think other-wise?). And my satisfaction and admiration seem limitless: I can't take my eyes off my new shoes. At certain moments, I stop and stare at these spotless, shiny black shoes that look so wonderful on me; I'm obsessed with their newness. They don't show the slightest sign of wear, not a single scratch. I look again at my perfect shoes, the sight of them fills me with joy; but then suddenly I notice a flaw, there's a flaw in their design, I'm sure of it (and I immediately look away), at the tip of my shoe (only one of the shoes has the flaw) (I can't ignore it), I have to concentrate if I want to for-get about it (the flaw). I must think about something else, must start again from zero and find a new pattern to impose upon my thoughts. I can see myself again on that day, frozen where I stand, incapable of forcing myself to carry on, and I understand that I am still somewhat sick. I don't see it very clearly, but I know there's a rupture in my mind, as barely noticeable as the flaw on my shoe (can I be blamed for having good eyes?), a fault that shouldn't be able to prevent me from continuing my walk, and I understand at this moment that what we call health is nothing more than a defense against a unified army made up of all the things that can lead us into despair. This is what I understand several weeks after leaving the hospital, and as soon as I realize this, a new perspective emerges in my mind: all of the details that have made up my new, unrestricted existence outside of the hospital's walls, which I've been persuaded until now were the purpose of my new existence, are now presented in a new light, a light marked by uncertainty that multiplies what I was feeling, like a group of dissonant notes struck on an out-of-tune piano. And I can no longer stop myself from noticing the dissonance. I'm in my bedroom and, I say to myself, I must pay close attention to every event (that occurs in my bedroom), I must be attentive and record each one of them in my notebook. Sitting on the ground, wearing only socks, I look at my shoes lying nearby and understand that from now on they are useless to me. The dissonant notes multiply and cascade around me (in the bedroom), I can't stop listening to them now. Since I've been in my bedroom (and since all preoccupation relating to my sickness has been banished from the field of my consciousness), I've been forced to listen to the tinkling of these notes, which are like grains of sand choking my mind's most fundamental machinery (the deepest and most subtle operations of my mind). I've started to think (watching the dissonant notes multiply) that my mental capacities, once maintained by the state of extreme concentration required by my sickness, abandoned me when I left the hospital, and that, by recovering my health, I lost in a single blow my ability to think and to form those cruel words upon which I'd once staked my entire future.

I see once again on Sauvage's face a certain movement that's not quite a reminder of impermanence, but which still somehow relates to time and speaks of time, of its obscure fate in the blood of the living, and whose progression can be described as a kind of obliteration; I search in the features of his indifferent face, marble-like and closed off to the temptations of the exterior world, for evidence of a curiosity painfully hidden beneath an excess of politeness and patience. I feel like a novice pilot on a reconnaissance mission, surveying from a low altitude an uncharted region that has just suffered the effects of a devastating flood; I can just barely make out through the dirty cockpit window the changes in the landscape: water has poured forth and invaded the plains, drowned the crops, the roads, the houses, has wiped out any trace of human life. It is not, however, the end of the world that I recount to Sauvage, nor even a theater of war, but rather an unfulfilled love. I describe to him my irreparable disaster (with love), my story of stagnation, my lost opportunity. Cathie is silent, enclosed in her bubble, and every evening I find her seated at the same place in the antechamber of hell (facing the screaming TV), and I explain to Sauvage how, using the careful cunning of a feline, I finally succeeded in approaching her. Sauvage watches me so calmly that I feel I might be misinterpreting the meaning of my own words, that what I think I'm saying is not what I'm saying in reality. And when I at last fall silent, disgusted with myself, either because it seems to me that I've reached the last degree of propriety or because I sense that boredom has taken hold, Sauvage, in turn, begins to speak; the prolonged silences that divide his speech are unlike anything I've ever known: sections of pure, abstract duration, shattered mountains of ice that crumble violently into the silencing expanse of water below. He talks about music and musical composition, and me, the complacent listener, seated by the telephone that never rings, I don't dare to interrupt. He tells me that he loves

music passionately, and that deprived of music, of the music
that has been his life's greatest consolation, he would be
unable to go on living. Seated (or lodged rather) in his
armchair, Sauvage claims to have studied musicology (and I
unquestioningly believe him), studies that allowed him to
develop and perfect his musical tastes, he says, lodged in his
armchair (while I sit directly across from him, seated in a
folding chair), and that at the same time irrevocably (and
mercilessly) destroyed (demolished, he repeats several times)
whatever taste he had for music (and above all for musical
composition). He evokes his musicological studies between
the peeling, yellow walls of his damp apartment, and I listen
to him describe with nostalgia his years of study while
watching the progressive deterioration of the wall. I can't take
my eyes off the wall's patches of mold, hovering in the
background like impenetrable toxic clouds, and I try to guess
the significance of these shapes (while Sauvage goes on
talking to me) and to understand the secret relationship that
exists between Sauvage's halted speech and the stains growing
throughout his apartment. He said: I had a taste for
composition (a great taste for it), and in my youth I must
have composed an incalculable number of scores (I believed
him), which I would lose interest in as soon as I had finished
them (he added). Anybody other than me, I thought at that
moment, would probably have shown a great deal of
skepticism when faced with Sauvage's claims, but the thought
didn't even occur to me, while listening to Sauvage, to doubt
his claims, and I imagined quite easily that he'd composed,
in his past (or in his youth, which amounts to the same
thing), an incalculable number of musical scores, driven by
restlessness or by determination (or some completely different
motive). A child, he said, is capable of anything, provided
that his parents believe in his natural dispositions, and as a
child I was also capable of anything, including composing
(he confirmed) from an extremely early age. I didn't doubt,

while he spoke to me sitting in his usual position (he never moved from his armchair, with its threadbare, worn-out armrests, I don't believe I ever saw him in any other position than seated in his chair), his claims, it never occurred to me to doubt his claims anymore than it occurred to me to doubt his existence, such as it was (that is, such as it was presented to me), always seated (or rather enthroned) (facing me), his elbows situated on the armrests of his chair, which reminded me of a specific type of chair I'd often seen at the hospital (though Sauvage's didn't have straps (or rubber wheels)). His parents, who had no musical training or even the slightest musical inclination (or even musical taste), had bought him a piano, which he immediately began to play (or, more specifically, which he immediately began to improvise on). He developed, from the first day he'd been given the piano, a talent for improvisation while also benefiting from lessons he was given by a neighborhood piano teacher, and Sauvage advanced so quickly that he was soon able to compose. Did he play his songs on the piano, did he compose for the piano? Not at all. He composed neither for the piano nor for any other musical instrument, he didn't compose with the goal of execution in mind but of the absolute (so to speak), he composed only for the pleasure of composition and he was thus able to compose for years in secrecy and for the sole benefit of his mathematical imagination (he was able to compose in complete tranquility and innocence, hidden away in his art) until the day his piano teacher discovered his talent for composition and advised him (or his parents rather) to enroll in a course for musical composition, which is where he found himself the next day, surrounded by other musicians. In less than two weeks, this course completely destroyed his taste for composition and killed (in less than two weeks) his mathematical imagination. It never occurred to me (to me, who listened to him with the fervor and devotion of a disciple) to doubt the word of Sauvage, who from the beginning I'd admired and considered as a kind of exceptional person stripped of his titles and powers or, to be more precise, as a sort of bishop or pope, the image of a pope eventually triumphing over the former (and implanting itself (implanting itself above all the other images aroused in me by the sight of Sauvage enthroned in his armchair)) after I'd seen in a book at the library a painting of Pope Innocent X by Francis Bacon (a painting that was an instant revelation for me) and had from then on been unable to rid my mind of the striking resemblance between Sauvage and the pope depicted by Francis Bacon (who had himself, I read in the same book, been inspired by a painting of the same pope by Velázquez). I returned several times to the library to verify his resemblance (which was for me a revelation) to Pope Innocent X (as depicted by Francis Bacon), and each time I confirmed (at the library, looking at the reproduction of *Study after Velázquez's Portrait of Pope Innocent X* by Francis Bacon) the striking resemblance between Sauvage and Bacon's pope, although I was totally incapable, once I found myself back in the presence of Sauvage (invariably seated across from me, his body leaning slightly forwards), of seeing the resemblance. As soon as I was sitting in front of Sauvage again (as I was almost every day), any comparison became impossible and my entire system of equation fell apart before the irrefutable exhibition of reality. What could there possibly have been in common between the imposing silhouette of Sauvage, whose body seemed to be imprisoned by the chair it never left (not under any pretext) (or more precisely: not under any pretext I'd ever seen), and that of the meager, agonized pope, shriveled up in his pontifical chair. I'd never seen Sauvage get out of his chair and I honestly believed he was incapable of moving his legs (not in the sense that he was truly (or physically) unable, but in the sense that he'd one day decided to forsake their usage): he seemed to me, who visited him every day, to be nailed into his chair in the same unmoving position as that of the pope sitting enthroned before the masses. Sauvage simultaneously defied the laws of movement and the laws of time, capable of remaining, as he claimed, in the same position for hours, his mind focused on some everyday object (any object could nourish his insatiable curiosity). He seemed to be the polar opposite (opposite in every way) of the pope Francis Bacon had painted several times throughout his life, and yet I still couldn't stop myself from comparing him (every time I saw him) to Pope Innocent X and being astonished by the resemblance. I eventually concluded that the association created by my mind between Sauvage and the pope was something of a miracle. That's it, I said to myself, it's a kind of miracle that gives rise to the image of Bacon's pope in your eyes, and you alone are witness to this miracle, confronted each day, or condemned (if you prefer), to contemplate the mysterious incarnation of Bacon's pope in the features of Sauvage. And each day I noticed that the only point in common between Sauvage and his double (who was in reality not his double, nor even a distant relative) was that they both seemed to be trapped for all eternity in their armchairs, the pope frozen (and immortalized) in a position imagined by Francis Bacon, and Sauvage fatally nailed to his chair by his corpulence and predisposition to inertia. And he didn't move on that day either, he made only a brief sketch of a movement that he retracted almost as soon as he'd started it (returning to his initial and fatal inertia and inviting me with a motion of his hand in the direction of his closet to look for the only composition he'd saved (of the many he'd written)). He composed simply because he had a taste for composition, he told me that day (as he did numerous other times), and though he considered himself in some ways a composer, he would never have compared himself (as a composer) to Webern, Schoenberg, or Górecki, his favorite composers, because his taste for composition was perfectly disinterested, to use his favorite expression. His admiration for Schoenberg and the others (he said), which was limitless, hadn't altered his taste for composition and hadn't dissuaded him from composing himself. He'd never compared himself to Webern (and the others), and fortunately he'd been spared the mania of comparison that eventually seizes every creator; though he had himself been a creator (a composer), he had somehow escaped this obsession. The smallest comparison, in this regard, would have been my annihilation, he said, annihilation of my desire to compose and annihilation of my own being, confronted as it would have been with its own insignificance. A pure and simple annihilation that mercilessly destroys anyone who experiences this need to compare and then eventually dies from this need, suffocated by their own unfathomable worthlessness. The best way to avoid comparing oneself to Schoenberg or Webern is to compose endlessly, without stopping to question the intrinsic value of the work (the notion of value had thus never hindered Sauvage's morale and the notion of judgment had never affected his capacity for production). If he'd ever taken the time to compare or evaluate himself, there's no doubt that he wouldn't have survived beyond the first minute, facing what would have certainly been a confirmation of his complete lack of talent. This idea that seizes all those who attempt to create something is fatal, and fortunately for him, the idea never once occurred to him in his youth (in his compositional youth), so far was the idea from his mind, in fact, that he began to consider himself as a true composer, and as long as he completed scores he never thought of evaluating himself, never asked himself if he was good or if he was bad. I had a habit of storing away my musical scores, he said, as soon as I finished them I stored them away (without exception) in an armoire, without ever once worrying about their musical value, perfectly indifferent as I was to their general (musical) value. And I imagined a young Sauvage, with a skinny silhouette, hurrying towards his armoire, a score in his hands. He piled each new score upon the last (he enjoyed having collections) and eventually the armoire literally broke apart under the weight of paper (of the kilos of scores), after several years it collapsed in the middle of the night and nearly killed him. To think, he said, that I could have died, smashed like a cockroach beneath the armoire that contained my entire musical oeuvre (all the musical material I'd ever composed). At the idea of ending up crushed under the weight of his oeuvre, whose value he never knew because he never thought of rereading his scores, Sauvage again experienced a visible satisfaction (visible especially to me, who was watching Sauvage with an intense and passionate curiosity), and the contentment he felt painted a disturbing grin on his face. And when I asked him to show me the scores (I was suddenly curious to see and feel one of these scores), he raised himself halfway out of his chair (pretending to try and free his massive body all while continuing to smile), but the movement was immediately aborted, as if he'd only wanted to create an illusion of mobility (just as the smile was meant to give an illusion of contentment). In reality, Sauvage hadn't had any intention of getting up and hadn't actually even moved, and yet I'd seen his movement, I hadn't hallucinated this movement which was impossible for Sauvage, who hadn't left his chair in years (or had left it as rarely as possible (on only the rarest of occasions) in all his years of immobility). He made a halfhearted motion with his hand in my direction, and, with his permission, I went to look for the score in the shoe closet. One day, shortly after his parents' death, he'd burned all the scores he'd stored at their house, he explained. When it was at last necessary to empty his parents' house (shortly after their death), Sauvage had felt a kind of disgust towards all the objects in the house (including his own scores, which were in some way part of the scenery (or setting) in which he'd learned to live and compose). All children must one day face this depressing task (emptying the house of their parents), and in doing so they all experience a profound disgust before the magnitude of this terrible and painful responsibility, which falls upon all children who survive their parents and consists of getting rid of their own parents' burdensome past, a past frozen like ice in the objects they once owned but which now take up too much space. The past of one's parents is a heavy lot, made up of miscellaneous objects that weigh on the conscience of the surviving children who suddenly and without having been prepared for it find themselves as the inheritors of a past that is not their own. That's how it is, said Sauvage, whose smile had subtly fossilized into an unnerving expression of despair, and the first blow brought by the death of one's parents, the first trial that death inflicts upon us, is not the fact that they are dead and gone forever, but that we must survive them (we, who are their children for the entirety of our lives) for an indefinite period of time. We always prepare ourselves in some way for the death of our parents (said Sauvage), I myself had prepared to confront this trial, which I dreaded more than anything else in the world (more than my own death) (which I also sometimes imagined, in diverse and usually dramatic forms), since I was a child, because no death seemed more horrible and unfair (and more insurmountable) to me than that of my parents, but in my heart I didn't think the worse would ever come, because the worst of all wasn't that they would die but that I would survive them. Sauvage's parents had died in an airplane accident in the territorial waters of Norway. He told me (on the subject on his parents) that since the beginning of their marriage they'd run a music shop. They, who could play no instruments and knew nothing about music, spent years selling musical instruments, and their business, which was not only profitable but prosperous, assured the small family a comfortable and easy life. It wasn't difficult to imagine that Sauvage had known a happy childhood, surrounded by his parents and all their instruments, and thus finding himself from the earliest part of his life, before the years of withdrawal and hiding (as he called his years of study), in the most favorable conditions, alone and sheltered from any form of judgment, for learning the art of music. Sauvage spent countless hours exploring the almost completely silent music shop, and no doubt his passion for composition was born in the silence of the store among all those noiseless instruments. He'd grown up and lived among the store's instruments, they were his childhood friends (to put it one way) (and his most loyal companions), and he never, throughout the course of his childhood (or later), felt ashamed of their secret companionship. Among the instruments displayed in the cabinets and hanging from the walls, he'd felt very early on an impulse towards musical enrichment, a desire to take part in the (musical) arts, which eventually ended, after years of study, in complete stagnation. In the company of timpani, violins, and horns, and all the other instruments that he never tired of contemplating and admiring, Sauvage cultivated an appreciation for silence and concluded that the most profound wish of music was to never be heard. Since his solitary childhood (in the vast store) he'd always associated music with silence, an association that had engraved itself onto his spiritually oriented mind, and every time after, throughout his life of solitude, that he found himself in an almost perfectly silent bedroom, he was overcome by the most profound joy, as if he'd been given a chance to hear the most beautiful music ever created. And finally I had the score in my hands, excavated carefully from the closet, but as I lifted it up, a photo escaped from its yellowed pages. It was the only souvenir he'd saved of his parents, Sauvage explained, as I bent down to recover the black-and-white photo from the floor. He couldn't say why he hadn't destroyed it with the others, why he'd been unable to separate himself from this particular photograph, which

showed Sauvage's father, still young, holding the equally
young mother of Sauvage by the shoulder (and in the short
time I had the photo in my hands, I immediately noticed the
striking resemblance between Sauvage and his mother), the
two of them standing in front of what must have been their
music store, smiling for the photographer (and smiling for
me, an impression that immediately made me feel ill at ease).
I found it difficult, while looking at the photo of Sauvage's
parents, to imagine that this young married couple relaxing
in front of their music shop could have been the parents of
Sauvage, and even more difficult to imagine that they'd been
the victims of an airplane accident; I couldn't envision the
man in the photo, holding his young wife's shoulder with
protective tenderness, in any other state of being than
standing next to his wife at the entrance of their music store,
both of them young and smiling, looking into the camera
with the discrete nostalgia of photographed beings. As one
always does while looking at photographs of people who have
disappeared (whether we knew them or not), I quietly
noticed and admired the secret bond the photographed have
with their own death, confronting the end with an
unparalleled degree of equanimity and courage, smiling
tranquilly to those of us who watch them (in the photo) from
the world of the living. Looking at the photo of Sauvage's
parents, I remember experiencing not only a sensation of
excusable indiscretion, but also thinking that people in
photographs always seem to confront death in an almost
tender fashion, and the photograph of Sauvage's parents
confirmed that tender, pathetic link between the living and
the death waiting for them someplace in their future.
Sauvage's parents died in an airplane crash in the territorial
waters of Norway during their first trip outside of the
territory of France. And Sauvage, like all children who from
one day to the next become survivors (survivors of their own
parents), had become disgusted with life and knew no other

way to continue his life than by selling off every last one of
his parents' possessions. Everything that had been theirs and
was now his (after the death of his parents) (or, if you like,
because of the very fact that they'd died) he burned, believing
that he was also burning some part of the suffering that had
resulted from their deaths. He sold the store and its
instruments, along with all the furniture in their house
(fifteen days after their funeral), and (at the same time and
in the same haste) he burned their papers and documents
because he couldn't live with the idea of someone seeing the
letters or photographs that had belonged to his parents, and
so he'd burned them all (or almost all), saving only one
photograph (out of all the others contained in the albums
he'd thrown into the fire) and one score (out of all the others
contained in the armoire that had been stuffed to its breaking
point with all sorts of miscellaneous objects) to serve as
witnesses of his happy childhood. And now, holding the score
in one hand and the photograph in the other, I couldn't
decide which one was more worthy of my attention. At that
moment, Sauvage was looking in a completely different
direction, his face turned towards the window (whose
existence, undoubtedly, was no longer registered by Sauvage),
and I said to myself (at that moment) that it wasn't in the
direction of the street that Sauvage was looking, but in the
direction of his own past, and I realized that I'd also ceased
to exist in his eyes. I began reading the score, now that
Sauvage's mind was elsewhere and I was freed from his
scrutiny, and curiously, though I'd never learned how to read
music, I began reading the score in question at full speed (the
tattered, secret score that had escaped the holocaust of
memories), not understanding at first how I could understand
it, but then realizing that the score beneath my eyes wasn't
filled with notes but with words and sentences, written out
in what I took to be Sauvage's handwriting. Sauvage looked
at me after a long period of silence (I'd finished reading

several minutes before and had said nothing) and asked me: So, what do you think? Excuse me? I said (I didn't know how to respond). What do you think? he repeated, to which I finally responded (after long consideration): I don't know, I really don't, and I explained to Sauvage that I didn't know how to read music. I see, he said incredulously, and, at that moment, I felt as if my embarrassed smile was separating my face into two warring tribes.

You must find a bedroom and never leave that bedroom once you've found it, I thought when I was once again alone. And in your bedroom, I thought again, you must calmly contemplate your life and tell yourself that, of all the possible lives, this is the life that was waiting for you and that all you must do is accept it, take it as it is, and stop dreaming of all the other possible lives. I went through my clothes, opened every one of my drawers to carefully check their contents, *checking for any error*, then moved automatically towards my desk, as if this was all part of my normal routine, and immediately thought of writing to Cathie, telling myself that the words were still there and I needed only to write them for Cathie to one day read them, that it wasn't even a question of knowing whether or not they truly existed but of having the courage to decide their fate by putting them down onto the page. This is why I've sat down here, I said to myself, stopping in the middle of a poorly begun sentence, having trouble recognizing my own writing (though it's my own hand that has written all this): to free these trapped words, which have become like empty shells to me, like the carcasses of dead insects. And I thought about those abandoned beach houses, deserted at the end of the summer, whose floors are covered with dead, dried-up flies, and I compared the words

I'd written to the morphology of the mummified insects, ideograms the color of ash, thinking about the influence of the flies and how I could overcome that influence. I have to admit that it's not always easy to live in such solitude. Fortunately, I have some possessions here to distract me. Sometimes, when the boredom becomes unbearable, I take an inventory of all these possessions, carefully weighing each object in my hands, admiring its voiceless resistance to time, its opacity. Every object that passes through my hands is a small mountain of silence and permanence, a world whose calm and fullness I envy. I must also admit that a bedroom can sometimes begin to resemble a prison. And misery, I say to myself in those moments when this resemblance is at its most noticeable, is not the prison or the state of being locked in a prison, but the thoughts of a man in a place that he calls a prison and takes for a prison, believing that he is there to purge whatever pain he may be harboring, thinking that he is there because circumstances required it and that he can change those circumstances at any moment to find himself someplace else.

And if I discover today that my life has been wasted, can I serenely contemplate my wasted life? Sitting on my bed, listening on a portable radio to the news of a world that seems to have no connection to my own life, I know that I am in need of calm, of simple, inoffensive thoughts about nothing in particular. These are the thoughts that can bring me a kind of temporary comfort, even if they often morph into complex, meaningless theories and end up spiraling uncontrollably through my mind like shooting stars (fleeting and capricious illuminations): scenes of the end of the world that embed themselves into my memory and return in the middle of the night, waking me up in a pool of sweat. My head then vibrates, full of strange words that throw a muddled light onto the remnants of my interrupted dreams. I laboriously try to put these words into some kind of order and then pronounce them in my head, searching for intelligibility and clarity, letting them stream by faster and faster, telling myself that you never know what you might find, what might come out of it in the end. And I tell myself that this could go on for a long time, each day repeating the events of its predecessor, each night a replica transplanted from the night before. And I tell myself then that I would like to have a new perspective of the world, *I would like to see the world from the viewpoint of fear*, to install myself permanently in the long, empty hours of boredom and watch the anomalies of the seasons outside my window, freed from emotion and an excess of fear: the final leaves of autumn, I tell myself, would reflect the mood of the situation in the network of their thin veins, clutching to their branches out of pure resentment, and I would rejoice in this spectacle for the entire morning, my mind empty, my moist forehead stuck to the windowpane. But fortunately I know that my notebook exists, my notebook which is a challenge against all the fear I've ever experienced, and that one day I'll have filled all of its pages and be able to move on, having nothing more to experience than the small, cruel joy of the end. But then one night I wake up and all these thoughts are in my head at once and I know that I won't be able to fall back to sleep, that there's nothing I can do, no point in staying in bed a second longer, I won't be able to shut my eyes for the rest of the night. I don't check my clock, I get up and get dressed, stumbling through the darkness of my cluttered bedroom, and at that moment I realize that I might be dreaming, and that if I'm not dreaming, I am at least behaving as if in a dream, moving with a heavy, inescapable slowness, like a blind man trying to find his way through an unfamiliar bedroom. And I fit easily into this dream, in fact, into the dream's fabric, watching the image of myself moving through the night in the cluttered bedroom, reacting to some secret signal that has forced me to get up. And I soon leave my unmade bed behind me, and I think about the man who will later discover this disorder when he returns to bed, knowing that although he'll disapprove of the mess he'll leave his thoughts unvoiced. Maybe I'll try to prolong this dream, I say when I find myself in the stairwell a little while later, a dream like a sentence one should never write or pronounce, not even to oneself, not even in a whisper, I say to myself with a shudder, but that one writes or pronounces anyway, all while foreseeing the disastrous consequences and problems it will bring to your coming actions, erasing any doubts on the subject of your future, that long hallway with the fading light that you will eventually have to cross. Why, as I feel the cold sting of the night on my face and hands, do I wish for this unpleasant dream to continue, *to continue at any price*? Must dreams be as untamable as wild animals? If so, I would like to drown them in a sack and let the memory of my crime fade from my conscience. It must be late in the night, maybe the sun will soon come up; outside the noises of day have begun, first faintly, then louder, as if the light has slowly given birth to the distinctions between things: the newspaperman's moped, for example, that I thought I'd heard, but even if I didn't hear him, it was good to get up anyway. My dream is simple, frighteningly simple: I'm with Sauvage, I meet him at some specific spot in the city and, although I can't recall the exact details of our conversation, I remember that at one moment he asks me a question whose meaning I understand just enough to say something resembling a response: I'm looking for a room, I tell him, and I illustrate my response with a vague gesture as he watches me with perplexity and even incredulity; he waits, and then finally he opens his mouth to say these words as an ambiguous smile takes shape on his face: *The bedroom you are looking for has never existed.* Then he turns around, steps away, and disappears. That's the end, and I know at that moment that if I've woken up and decided to leave my bedroom, it's to go find him in that same street and to try to understand what he meant as he stared at me with his deranged eyes. I know that my chances of finding him are infinitesimal, and even if I persuade myself to try anyway I'm not in the slightest bit confident that he would deign to acknowledge me. I know that a dream is a dream and means very little, and I know that a street you see in a dream, even if the street is a real street in a real city, is most likely a misleading sign, and I know as well that when a real city begins to resemble a city from a dream, it's your own errant mind that should be blamed for the deception and not the indifferent city that surrounds you. And so, filled with indecisiveness regarding my own actions and my chances of finding Sauvage, I turn back on my path and go up the stairs, trying to smother the sounds of my steps the whole way up. Why must I behave as if my most insignificant actions could incriminate me?

It's true that Sauvage's behavior, now that I think back on our relationship, could have been called strange: immobile, unsmiling, the rare words that escaped despite his preference for silence, most often murmured, and which I took as signs of encouragement, as if he was urging me to go on with what I was saying, but which could also have been interpreted as a warning, a suspicion, a hostility; like the day I was telling him about the circumstances in which I thought I'd seen Cathie again, and Sauvage held out his hand to me and said, barely moving his lips, Cathie is not who you think she is. I still don't know what he meant by this or if he really even

said it, and I have no idea what I should have understood if
he really had said it. I thought I'd seen Cathie in the munic-
ipal library I'd been visiting regularly for several weeks. I'd
had difficulty deciding whether or not it was really her, I said
to Sauvage, and my uncertainty became disgust when I realized that I hadn't recognized her because her smile had disappeared. Her smile was gone, lost somewhere inside her
pale, emotionless face, but I would have given anything to
see it one more time, I thought, searching her innocent face
for some remnant of that smile. She was seated two tables
down, turned slightly away from me, and I was struck immediately by her elegance. She was feverishly flipping through
the pages of a book, as if looking for a specific passage or
sentence, yes, I was sure she was looking for some precise
piece of information, though it was impossible to say exactly
what. Nothing seemed to exist in the space around her, I
could see that immediately, and as I considered that I myself
might also not exist for her, I found that all my repressed fury
had begun to return. There was a bright-red jacket folded
over a neighboring chair, in which I hadn't yet noticed anything threatening or worthy of attention, I didn't understand
that it also had a role to play in all this, perhaps even the
starring role. At that instant, I said to Sauvage, as I felt my
fury rising more powerfully within me, a demonic jack-in-
the-box suddenly sprung center stage, I understood nothing
about the jacket or its power, but I was all the same fascinated
by the sight of Cathie, her face bent over the book with a
glimmer of purpose in her eyes as she flipped crisply through
its pages with a disturbing efficiency. I looked away for just
a moment, and when my eyes fell back on Cathie the jacket
was already over her shoulders and she was tearing a page
from the book; she then folded the page and placed it into
the pocket of her jacket, all without a single glance around
her or a second of hesitation, no, she wasn't trying to conceal
her theft from anyone. And at that moment, without

knowing why, I felt simultaneously that I was a coward and
that I needed to carry out some inexplicable revenge, perhaps
for the stolen page, but probably for some more obscure
reason: that page, I would tell Sauvage, was only a diversion,
its smooth, gleaming surface hiding a reality more compli-
cated, more troubling, and more sinister than anything I was
yet aware of. Because of this suspicion then, and because I
was now part of an experiment whose outcome could only
condemn me, push me further into despair, I followed her
into the street, hypnotized by the menacing red jacket. This
piece of clothing hanging from Cathie's shoulders, and con-
forming snugly to the shape of her waist, irrefutably proved
to me that she'd become capable of denying, with the entirety
of her red-dressed being, her past, her virtues, her difficultly
recovered mental health; I imagined her leaving the hospital
and forgetting everything about her stay, suffering complete
amnesia because of her elegantly cut jacket. To be honest, it
could have been another girl entirely, but something in me
was crying out that the truth no longer mattered: it was
Cathie, a Cathie that I didn't know, that I'd never thought
possible, and that, for this reason, I had to follow. Her life
has changed thanks to this piece of clothing, I thought, seeing the evidence in the smooth, confident movements of her
perfectly functioning body; but don't worry, I thought spite-
fully, this can't go on for long, and then I don't know what
happened, a pebble beneath my shoe or a lapse of nerve, but
I tripped and nearly fell to the ground, all while keeping my
eyes in her direction for fear of losing sight of her. I wanted
at any cost to find out the address of the melancholic red
jacket, I told Sauvage to justify my behavior, and so I followed her, the woman I took to be Cathie, an alternative
Cathie who had developed the elegance of an actress, I
wanted to engrave her address into every compartment of my
memory, to be able to say at what address this red jacket,
which was the cause of my humiliation and which I've been

unable to forget ever since, lived. I admit that I felt pathetic as I began guessing the reasons for her sudden departure: perhaps she'd wanted to avoid me because of my second-hand clothing, or maybe something else about me had filled her with fear, fear most likely aroused from a single glance in my direction, a glance that shoved her backwards into a past of confusion and regret. I immediately assumed that the jacket must have cost her a great sum of money, unless she'd stolen it from some luxury boutique, and I imagined that Cathie had all at once become extravagant, frivolous, and a thief, picturing Cathie's metamorphosis as she walks down the street, trying to seduce everyone she passes, delighting in the stares she attracts from strangers, strutting everywhere with her audacity, her insolent confidence, in parks, in stores, wearing the red jacket that betrayed everything I'd thought I'd known about her, the girl I'd never seen dressed in anything other than a bathrobe or a nightgown. And now that she was walking in front of me, just several meters away, I told myself to keep walking, do not stop for anything, I repeated to myself, although I felt that my thoughts would never be able to join those of Cathie, up ahead on the stage of her little red theater. Cathie isn't who you think she is, Sauvage said again, interrupting my story. He pronounced the words with an implacable firmness, as if to cut short a story whose ending he already knew, and then held out his hand to me in a gesture I didn't at first understand. Silently, I watched the slow advancement of his hand, sensing that something was about to be revealed. Sauvage's hand wasn't empty, it cradled a miniature Russian doll with blond hair and red cheeks. I watched the doll for a moment, searching in her frozen stare for a response, an answer, while Sauvage, completely silent, could barely hide his satisfaction. He has just achieved some sort of victory, I thought at that moment, and me, I've just lost something, something whose importance I hadn't suspected and whose absence will certainly come back to haunt me later, something he's removed from me forever, I thought while watching the curious sight of the miniature lacquered doll in Sauvage's massive hand. Now, when I remember this scene, I experience an inexplicable feeling of sadness and shame, and for a long time to come I'll remember the hand that seemed to suddenly detach from Sauvage in order to breach the distance between us, a hand that didn't seem to belong to his body, as if it had been given a life of its own right before my very eyes, and even before the eyes of Sauvage, who didn't seem to entirely understand what he was doing himself. And there, in the palm of his hand, undeniably, it wasn't the Russian doll that I now saw but Cathie herself, or rather her effigy, her essence. Cathie, whom I'd tried everything to see again, and who had driven me out of my bedroom, was rolling in Sauvage's hand like a nutshell in the ocean, for weeks now she'd been a prisoner of his hand, cupped in its moist shadow, hearing our muffled voices and perhaps trying to guess what kind of game was being played out between us.

I want to talk to you about a notebook—the notebook in which I've started writing all of this. It's one of the few objects in my life towards which I feel an attachment. In fact, it wouldn't be an exaggeration to say that this notebook is my only possession, my only piece of property (so to speak). I've managed to keep it all this time, I'm amazed it hasn't been lost or destroyed. I have it in front of me now that night has fallen, and I'm writing in it under the beam of a flashlight (the power cuts out here frequently). Maybe you know this: men, like the streets of a city, have names, and they carry those names wherever they go, and every man who knows his own name can think of that name as a kind of light that illuminates the darkness of his thoughts and actions. *You can change the name of a street*, give it whatever name you want, and no one will notice any difference after the name has been changed. And I, who have so much trouble finding my way around in this city, where I feel more and more like a stranger to myself, I carry this notebook with me everywhere I go, as evidence, as proof of who I am. It's a school notebook with about a hundred pages (ninety-six to be exact), a notebook (standard size (17x22 cm)) whose light green cover is wrinkled and stained, a notebook that has surely seen better days. I found it behind an armoire a long time ago, in the apartment I was then renting. I brought it back to life in some sense (in the middle of the night), it existed once again, more real than it had ever been before: I could touch it, flip through it, handle it like a treasured object, imagine its story, its destiny, its misadventures in the hands of another. I can go back (with this notebook as my guide) to that distant time, when every newly discovered object plunges me into a world of complex thoughts and reasoning. I don't know how or when I picked up this habit, but every morning, as soon as I wake up, I drop a probe at random into some part of my mind and begin to monitor my thoughts. Attentive to the slightest stirrings of my mind, I note down and interpret one by one the signs of my present condition through the manifestation of my thinking, and I don't realize right away the seriousness of my state, I don't know that the signs I'm seeing are symptoms characteristic of a *sick state of being*. I see nothing coming, I can't see the fracture, completely concentrated as I am on reading my thoughts as if they were coffee grounds. I lead an isolated life in an unusual and depressing apartment, located in a run-down neighborhood. The neighborhood of ancient construction, as it's called, and which despite its name seemed to be perpetually under construction, or even worse: it seemed that the construction would never be completed, that the neighborhood and its development had been forgotten and would go on forever ignored, filled with unwanted buildings and outcast inhabitants existing together in a state of eternal abandonment. A neighborhood that was beyond comparison, that was unlike any other neighborhood in the world. My apartment: extremely narrow (in an old building), not unlike a hallway, with an absurdly high ceiling, perhaps five or six meters tall. This apartment, which consisted of a single, elongated room that held the bedroom, living room, a small kitchen, a wardrobe, and a miniature bathroom, was where I made my home. I spent a great deal of time seated on my bed, with nothing to do or to distract me. I felt no need to do anything, to use my time in any meaningful way. All things considered, I felt neither boredom nor restlessness. Any notion of ambition had vanished from the horizon; I don't know why I'm here or why I never get bored, I often said to myself. Whenever I went out, it was always at the same time and for the same reason. I knew my walking route by heart, repeating it identically each day; I could have run through those streets blindfolded. And they all began to look the same in the end, straight and depressing, like an endless hallway under the steel-gray light of October. I'd started, I think, to understand what the unhappiness of a man can be: to have only one city and to know that this one city is made up of a finite number of streets. I believe I'd fallen prey to melancholy, to the complications of an evolving illness, a complex form of melancholy that had anchored itself to me, an undefined form of melancholy that was coming back, stronger and stronger, with each passing hour.

Sitting next to my window, watching raindrops run along the glass, I can see us again in his room, the daylight quickly

fading away. I remember that long winter filled with talk of
Cathie, our empty glasses sitting before us late into the night:
Sauvage and I, driven by the same fervor, by the same impatience and insatiable curiosity (emotions ready to explode
inside us like live grenades) that made us sometimes cheerful,
talkative, and vulnerable, sometimes bitter, depressed, and
even more vulnerable to sadness, reacting in the same ways
to the same words, searching each other's sentences for a sign
or a clue, the shadow of Cathie always in the background,
always out of reach. Often, when I began speaking about her
without any thought of self-restraint, it seemed to me that
Sauvage would lend a great deal of attention to my words,
although he usually seemed determined to persuade me of
the contrary by hiding himself behind a mask of indifference
(the mask of a distant Sauvage, half-awake or even completely
asleep) (and affected by nothing) that I'd learned with time
to understand, to appreciate without analysis, as one might
a painting. And every day, or rather every evening, I watched
him, half-protected and half-exposed by the weak light of his
desk lamp, wondering to myself if this light, which so poorly
illuminated his face and his movements, might have been
meant to unsettle me, just like the unchanging, seemingly
calculated arrangement of his books and notes sometimes
unsettled me; every evening I felt as if I was taking part in
a ceremony whose meaning was invariably lost on me but
whose final revelations I went on secretly awaiting. More
than once it seemed like I was on a much too narrow stage,
surrounded by a set that had been meticulously arranged and
lacked any chairs or superfluous props, any of the expected
accessories of real life (a life that went on all the same, continuing to beat in the hearts of all the other tenants in the
building, beyond the walls of the living room), as if more
space would give our performance a greater chance of being
carried out. I was sure, on more than one occasion, that I
was acting in a play written for two characters, Sauvage and

I sitting face to face in a sort of undefined and inept combat, made all the more frightening because I couldn't guess what was at stake or how it could possibly end; we confronted each other like two actors of unequal talent, one (Sauvage) sure of his lines, his ability, the other (me) inexperienced, overwhelmed by anxiety, embarrassed by his movements and uncomfortable in his elocution: this battle would end like every battle, I thought, in defeat and humiliation, unless a surprise or miracle appears at the very last moment, a miracle, I thought, that would also be a sort of twilight for our most secret intentions. In Sauvage's living room, which was no longer really a living room but a theater built for the acting out of a scene we'd by then repeated many times, I knew that our words had lost all relationship with reality, all ambition to even mimic reality: not only could they not be heard by anyone else, they were no longer even meant to be understood by the two of us who pronounced them. I'd like to remember Sauvage exactly as he was, but I know that memory is a light that always casts shadows in certain places and that on the memory of Sauvage there are shadows that are the *consequence* of the light. To better remember him do I have to first separate the shadows from the light? Aren't the shadows that fall on the people we remember themselves a kind of light, destined to unveil their true face? Sauvage, despite his curiosity, often fell asleep (or often seemed to) in the middle of conversations, and sometimes, even as I pronounced the first words of a sentence in my trembling voice, he would seem to have fallen deaf, and as I entered into the heart of a subject, he began to appear truly overcome with fatigue, his attention fading further and further away until he showed only intermittent evidence of life, as if his mind was occupied entirely with something else, and I reasoned that only the sound of his own voice could keep him awake and give his heavy, seated carcass some appearance of life and mobility. It was in moments like this that Sauvage would take shelter behind his black sunglasses, claiming a sudden sensation of optic sensitivity. A cold-blooded animal, I thought more than once of Sauvage, hiding his true self somewhere deep within his massive body while exuding his malaise in regular, carefully calculated doses, his sunglasses opposing like a plea of inadmissibility all attempts to probe his thoughts. I'd noticed that every time he fell quiet, either because I'd begun to speak, encouraged by I don't know what to break suddenly out of our silence, or because he'd requested some record for us to listen to, it was as if Sauvage had been switched off, losing all signs of life, lucidity, and awareness, sliding towards sleep along an irresistible slope whose different stations I'd by now seen many times, starting at polite, vaguely encouraging silence and ending in the deepest and most perfect entrenchment. But still I would go on talking to him, spurred on perhaps by a desire to win his attention, to stir the troubled waters of his inner self, to discover if there was any part of this exhausted man's mind that could still be reached. He seemed imperturbable in those moments, and (curiously) attentive to the conversation, to the course of the conversation (without beginning or end), or rather of an uninterrupted monologue taking place in some sense without him, although the respiration of the enormous mass of flesh sitting before me, rising and falling with each breath, was proof that he was really there (facing me), and maybe even more present than he might at first have seemed, truly (though secretly) attentive to the meaning of my words. Could he really have been sleeping? And if he was, did my words have any chance of reaching him? I imagined that he had the power to withdraw entirely into himself, into a secret and icy den, where daylight couldn't penetrate, and where, sheltered from all judgment, he could continue to nourish his insatiable curiosity. And I hoped to discover the entrance to this safe room, which nobody other than Sauvage had the right to enter. Nothing could stop me from talking about Cathie, without tact, without restraint, and with such assurance that I sometimes felt I was lying to both Sauvage and myself, the most important thing, confronted with a sleeping Sauvage, being to find a way to reawaken his attention.

It's an understatement to say that Cathie had fascinated him; perhaps, I'd begun to think, she'd even seduced him, capable as she was of exercising her charm on anyone who happened to hear about her; and I could do nothing against it, on the contrary, I only knew how to worsen the wound, sick at the idea that they might one day meet. Although Sauvage often spoke of the advantages of solitude (he could pretend all he wanted), I was beginning to suspect that he'd stopped believing his own words. Looking into his concentrated face, I could see his impatience and his efforts to conceal (with great difficulty) that impatience, yes, I said to myself, so much effort to try and hide something that was hardly even still a secret, that was ready to be revealed at any moment, I was sure he wouldn't delay much longer in putting his cards on the table, and when he does, I said to myself, I would learn what it truly means to lose. I knew it, I was completely sure of it, now that I could better recognize the signs and had learned how to read them on Sauvage's face. A gesture sufficed to put a stop to our endless dialogues, and I would then place Górecki's record on the player. The symphony would begin and then rise softly in successive waves through the darkness of the small room, and we would feel neither the need nor the ability to mutter another word. As the silence went on, rendered almost solid by the surrounding shadows, I couldn't suppress the thought that I was no longer useful for anything, that it was too late for me to start my life again, and I remembered, while listening to the ominous sound of the double basses, how alive I'd felt around Cathie. And what was Sauvage thinking about as I drove back into the darkness of my memory? He seemed to be absent: did he know that you can't change your life, that human behavior, in both the broad strokes and the details, is as rigorously predetermined as the notes on a score? Everyone is the same, Sauvage began to say that evening, once the room had become silent; everybody wants to be happy, imagines that they were born to live a happy life, he said, and I thought at that moment that Sauvage, as every man does, must also have once believed in the possibility of happiness, but had then become disillusioned with this dream. I instinctively lowered my eyes away from his, and something whispered inside me that he wasn't being sincere, that he was trying to deceive me or even harm me. And, he continued, when it happens that nature gives birth to someone different from the average human being, a human who is not born to be happy but, on the contrary, seems to have been born to be miserable, then this mortal being immediately represents an enigmatic threat to the human species. And because of the danger and mystery he represents for the rest of humanity, this mortal being's only possibility for survival is to isolate himself and conceal his instinctive misery in his deepest recesses. Cathie is not of this world, he let out at last, after a long look in the direction of the door, as if she might walk in at any moment, and I couldn't stop myself from also looking towards the door, hoping and waiting for the first signs of a resolution. He'd always known that Cathie had belonged to a place beyond the ordinary world, and that, according to him, was why I'd fled from her, because I'd been overcome by fear. The world in which Cathie lived was not the world of unanimous aspiration for happiness, but the world of misery, and I'd lacked the courage to join that world, I'd been a coward and let

fear get the best of me, I hadn't understood that fear only
has the power we give it ourselves: fear, he would say, like a
dog, needs a master, not a servant. Cathie didn't belong to
the normal world, she was unlike anyone else and shared no
resemblance to any other human being (in this world), this
is what he'd been waiting to tell me as we listened to the last
notes of Górecki's symphony, to make me understand that
I'd lost everything because of fear.

I'd picked up the habit (curiously without difficulty) (in
masking my efforts) of steadily following the flow of my
thoughts in Sauvage's presence, accustomed to the outbursts
and, even more so, to the persistent silence (of Sauvage),
which I no longer interpreted as a rejection or an insult. He
seemed to sleep peacefully and guiltlessly, taking refuge in the
inaccessible zone behind his sunglasses, whereas for myself,
I'd given up on trying to cross that border, and I no longer
wondered if his behavior was a sign of profound interest or
of an even profounder withdrawal, and I noticed that I'd
begun to talk in a curious, almost breathless voice, as if I was
concentrated (extremely concentrated) and at the same time
detached from my own body, when speaking to him about
Cathie, speaking endlessly in an almost inaudible whisper,
with no thought of restraint or the consequences of the next
day. And Cathie, since I'd begun recounting the smallest
details of our story, had no doubt taken an exceptional and
enigmatic place in Sauvage's mind. When I think about it
today, from the sobering distance of memory, I realize that
Sauvage must have felt towards Cathie, whom he'd never met
but nevertheless must have felt he at least knew a little ((if not
completely) (as if he'd actually met her, he said, and known
her independently of me)), and whom he would like to get to

know better by eventually meeting her, an innocent interest born from his intellectual curiosity (according to his own terms), and for all I know, this interest tore through Sauvage's life with the crushing force of a cyclone. For some time, I explained to him that day, I'd circled around her without daring to actually approach her, advancing with muted steps, with a kind of superstitious restraint, because I'd immediately understood that I wouldn't reach her without first crossing the borders of the progressively narrow concentric circles that surrounded her, jumping from one circle to the next with the cautious agility of a cat. I was somewhat distrusted at the hospital because I refused, due to either pride or indifference, to participate in the bargaining and transactions that regulated the daily exchange of cigarettes, condoms, and telephone cards, I sometimes even feared that I might be transferred for my failure to conform. It thus took me several weeks to reach the invisible, but nevertheless real, edge of the final circle, in the noise and violence of the TV room, where the news channel looped over and over. I'd followed her into this room, which was assiduously avoided by the other patients, no longer trying to conceal myself from her, and I watched the news unflinchingly, just like her. What was she really waiting for in there? Was she also waiting, as I was, for the end of the world? On the day she finally noticed me, I swore that it felt as if she'd set everything up herself, and that if we'd both happened to find ourselves there, together in the same place, it wasn't because I'd wanted it but because she'd been able to foresee the necessity of the roles we had to play in each other's lives, and everything that happened after, that evening and in the evenings to come, I accepted without any particular surprise or rejection or approval, like a series of painstakingly planned and inevitable events, like a decision made long ago. I'd crossed the final circle, and at the precise moment that my face was approaching hers, she began to smile, and this soft, detached smile all at once cleared up an ambiguity and cast a shadow over my thoughts. She was sitting right there next to me, and although I'd kept my eyes wide open, I could no longer see anything or think anything, I was surrounded by darkness, trapped, more alone than ever before, with only a memory of the smile that had been the reward for all my efforts. I can see her face again, bathed in the raw, violent light flowing out of the TV. I can see her surprise, and I realize that her smile, sincere and uncorrupted by her surroundings, wasn't meant for me and asked for no interpretation. I'm trying right now to find the right words, and I look inside myself for them in the hope that they will help me find meaning in my life, which I now realize I almost lost in the night; a believer opens to the first pages of the Bible, in moments of extreme terror or humiliation, sensing the approach of something inescapable and seeking to interrogate his fate and probe his own heart before facing some great decision (to beat on, to cease), because he believes that the words are spelled out clearly somewhere in the book, that they've been dictated by providence with this precise moment in mind, and precisely because he attaches so much meaning to that which is written, this man is blind. And like any man ready to tie his destiny to a set of words, I think of Hamsun's novel and am immediately convinced that Hamsun's words were written for this moment, so that I could live in this moment exactly as it was meant to be lived in, in all its darkness and uncertainty, words written not to give me a glimmer of hope, but, on the contrary, to help me close my mind to any thought of redemption.

How to chase from one's mind an image of an empty armchair, to erase the fear aroused by a vision? I think I'm in need of the peace that comes from a dreamless night, to feel

again the calmness of knowing that your thoughts are
completely under your own control. Time always seems so
long, so full of bitter silence, as monotone as a yellow rain
that floods the countryside and erases the names written on
the entrance signs of villages. I have to find a strategy, to
devote some time to deciding how to best regain my strength.
While waiting, I run through my memories, and this
armchair, which I see again in the middle of an empty room,
I can remember every last detail of it. And I also see Sauvage,
on the day before his departure, impassive, seated in his chair,
telling me that he's moving. He doesn't offer me a seat, he
has to go (the following day) (at dawn), he announces from
the depths of his chair. He speaks calmly, as always, he doesn't
say what's made him decide to leave, though he must have
his reasons, I say to myself, he has his reasons for not telling
me his intentions. The silence of a man is always preferable,
I think as I watch him, preferable to any explanation that
would tarnish his decision; it's in silence that one must
confide the secrets of one's actions, whereas words can do
only one thing: throw doubt upon the mind, corrupt the
impact of our decisions. I thought at first that Sauvage had
brought his translation to completion, that's what I
immediately thought, that he'd finished translating the
dictionary of rare and incurable diseases and was now ready
to move on, he had no reason to stay in his run-down
apartment now that the translation was complete. And as for
me, I was going to find myself alone again, isolated in my
bedroom, more alone than ever before, I would have to
relearn how to live by myself, to better handle my solitude,
and I wondered how many days would have to pass before I
would be able to accept my loneliness as I once had. A new
life was beginning for Sauvage, who was suddenly unbound,
freed from responsibility, while I was going to have to restart
my life from zero, for me a new life was beginning also, but
it would be one without grandeur, without destiny, because

I hadn't yet decided what to do with myself, and I wasn't sure if I would be able to face the life waiting for me tomorrow, two floors above in my furnished bedroom. How had I been unable to interpret the signs leading up to his departure? The possibility of him leaving hadn't even crossed my mind, I thought, scolding myself for my unforgivable ignorance, my intolerable lack of insight. I began to listen more attentively to Sauvage's voice, which was explaining that he'd made the decision to move and nothing could stop him from carrying out that decision now that it was made, but I could no longer recognize the sound of his voice, it had become the voice of someone else, an imposture that had taken Sauvage's place and was now commanding Sauvage's movements and will. I didn't recognize the voice that was announcing the departure of Sauvage and making a mystery of his destination, and I realized that my intelligence was useless facing the enigma of Sauvage and that even if I'd been the cleverest of men, my cleverness would be worthless in trying to unravel Sauvage's secret intentions. The only thing I was certain of at that moment, and of which I was suddenly very certain, was the confusion that had taken hold in my head, a confusion that no amount of reasoning would have been able to set straight. He wouldn't change his mind about his decision, I knew it, and he wouldn't justify it either, and I had to accept his inexplicable decision, and I told myself I should feel fortunate that he'd decided to tell me about it at all. Before making an irrevocable decision, it's a man's way of speaking that changes first, not his behavior. It's a man's silences, I said to myself, that must be understood to predict his disappearance. And I remembered that Sauvage hadn't spoken of illness for some time, hadn't even pronounced the word illness, and the absence of the word illness in my final conversations with Sauvage should have caught my attention, should have alerted me, I thought to myself. Sauvage was going to leave, to some place faraway no doubt, his arrangements were made and his decision was closed to appeal, as clear and sharp as the blade of a knife, and I'd seen nothing coming. The first change in a man, when he has resolved to do something that will change his life forever, something that cannot be undone, is in the silence that replaces his conversation, the words which he no longer pronounces. And if you really want to hear this man, I thought, hear what he's really saying at the moment he says it, to understand him from beginning to end, it's his silences that must be listened to. Sauvage hadn't mentioned illness for some time, hadn't lectured on the theme of fatal illness or cited the name of a single disease, all while I'd been unable to stop thinking about illness, to stop my thoughts from revolving entirely around the subject. Nothing could stop him now, I was certain that this would be the last time I would ever see Sauvage, it was the disappearance of the word illness that made me so sure, I couldn't lie to myself, I was certain that Sauvage was going someplace far away and would never come back from that part of the world where illness doesn't exist and where the word and the symptoms of the word illness and its multiple declinations are useless. Sauvage had been cured of the word illness, he'd become healthy, I said to myself, and he was getting ready to join a part of the world unknown to me, while I had revived my relationship with illness, had forged impossible connections with illness and death, to the point that I no longer felt capable of making even the smallest effort to leave my bedroom. I was so obsessed with illness that I hadn't noticed any change in Sauvage's conversation and attitude, and while his entire attitude suggested that he was free from any preoccupation with illness, I'd seen nothing and had sunken, without realizing it, further into illness, I'd begun to drone on and on about illness and I hadn't even noticed it. I was now watching his calm, unmoving silhouette (the (unchanging) silhouette of Sauvage) detach itself from the yellow wall that had so often served as the backdrop for

our discussions, and I saw that the dictionaries had
disappeared from his desk. There was no question that he'd
been cured of the word illness and his preoccupation with
illness, I said to myself when I'd noticed the disappearance
of the dictionaries that had helped him in his work and in
his subtle distinguishing of the word illness. Illness had
ceased to exist in both his mind and his dictionaries, and also
in any other part of his room, and soon Sauvage himself
would no longer be in the room that had once contained all
this, contained not only his physical being (and his mental
obsession), but his books and dictionaries as well. What had
he done with the dictionaries? I wondered. With a quick look
around the room, I verified that his shelves were entirely
empty. The dictionaries and all the science contained within
the dictionaries (as he often said) had already disappeared
from the room, they weren't on the shelves or the desk or
anywhere else in the room, so then where had he put them,
I asked myself, those heavy, priceless dictionaries, how had
he managed to make them disappear? Because I didn't believe
he was even capable of getting out of his armchair or carrying
a cardboard box, no, I couldn't even imagine him standing
up on his own two legs, and yet there was no other possibility
and I began to imagine the scene, not in order to understand
it or derive any conclusions from it, but simply to imagine
it, to admit to myself that he must have thrown everything
out the window, letting the science and the dictionaries fall
to the ground from his room on the ninth floor. Thousands
of pages thrown out the window in the middle of the night
on a sudden impulse, and maybe with those thousands of
dictionary pages he'd also thrown the completed and polished
manuscript of rare and incurable diseases, the giant
dictionary, translated and corrected, maybe reread one final
time before being thrown out of the window and into the
night, I imagined while watching Sauvage's silhouette,
sharply carved out by the backlight coming in through the

window. I can picture him quite clearly, Sauvage, bent out the window, proudly facing the sleeping city alone, maybe whispering some final words before throwing everything out, without regret, without the slightest hesitation, thinking (or rather screaming): good-bye illness, then closing the window and smiling at what he'd done. When he speaks about life from now on, I thought, he will use the word life and no other word, in his new life Sauvage will say life and not be tempted to pronounce the word illness or any other word in its place. He will keep the imperishable memory, hard as a diamond, of the night when he finished his translation and freed himself from his torment, and every time he pronounces (or writes) the word life, his satisfied expression will reflect the rain of manuscript pages thrown into the void. In Sauvage's vocabulary, I thought, illness is not a missing word, or even a catastrophic memory to be purged, but a window open to the night. I knew that I would never see him again as we sat silently in his living room, I was certain that everything had been said, that another word would only deepen the silence. And I looked over the room, patiently, very slowly, knowing it would be the last time I would see it, mentally photographing the smallest details for storage in my memory, this room that had been emptied of everything that had once darkened it and that seemed now to be bathed in a cold, bright light, almost dazzling, and Sauvage himself, I noticed, seemed suddenly lost inside the immensity of his armchair.

In the darkness of his room, I say to myself now, Sauvage's obsession had taken its time, slowly but steadily growing like a tenacious species of plant, scornful of the wall it has chosen as its home, thriving in all climates and conditions, resistant to frost, to the changes of the seasons, to storms, to floods; and I, who had foreseen nothing, who couldn't even have imagined what was happening, had done nothing to stop its growth. Sauvage had hidden his obsession for a long time, he'd tucked it away somewhere deep within his heart and covered it with a bed of stones, left it buried and forgotten until the evening, when, unable to go on holding it back, he finally let everything come out. Incurable diseases had stopped interesting him for some time, but I'd noticed nothing, not yet suspecting the metamorphosis of the man I'd been visiting every day, seemingly unchanged, solemn and frozen in his armchair; and yet, I say to myself now, I could have been more alert, I should have noticed that Sauvage had been behaving differently, absent from himself as if preoccupied by some anxiety that was subtly transforming the features of his face. And at this late hour in the poorly lit living room, the day before his departure, his words had become intoxicating, it was as if I'd been electrified by the sound of his voice, rendered mute by the sudden nervousness emanating from him as he tried to open his soul to me and speak for the first time about Cathie; but not the Cathie I'd known at the hospital, he explained as he turned his eyes away from mine, seeming to look towards some far-off place, as if from behind the lenses of his sunglasses he could see something visible only to himself, the future or some promise of resolution, and I understood that he'd waited a long time for this moment and that nothing could stop him now from saying everything he meant to say. His ideas about Cathie had come to him immediately, he'd put together, as he said to me, a true picture of Cathie, whom he was now convinced he knew better than anyone else, and especially better than me, who had only known her at the hospital, a declaration I couldn't accept but which I nevertheless lacked the courage to refute. Life is poorly designed, he began to say. Poorly designed for the empty man incapable of tolerating his own emptiness. A man who cannot live alone, cannot even begin to put up with himself, and so is willing and eager to attach himself to anyone, ready to settle down anywhere, under a pretext of love or friendship, with the single goal of consoling his own solitude. Every man strives to banish solitude from his life, and when this banishment cannot be carried out, he drags into his failure a friend or a woman who will allow him to forget his solitude. This friend or woman, who becomes indispensible to the man's survival, has only one role to play: to annihilate the man's solitude and oversee its complete destruction. But misery demands that each time he tries to escape his own darkness, the forsaken man enters an even blacker darkness, against which he collides and shatters his bones. I'd met the vital other, he told me, and to my own detriment, I'd thrown myself into her, had tried to absorb the darkness that was inside her and, also to my own detriment, had thought I'd cured my own solitude by plunging into a night darker than my own, but I hadn't gone to the end of this night, I'd turned back too early and retaken the path towards light, and now everything was irrevocably lost and my life was more purposeless and empty than ever before. I'd certainly met the vital other in my beloved Cathie, but I hadn't known that the vital other demands impossible efforts, and I hadn't truly loved her, the woman who could have changed my life forever but whom I hadn't followed to the end of the night; and my life from now on would be defined by my regret for having missed what could have changed it, Sauvage said, deciding that on this night he would leave nothing unsaid. A new encounter is a disaster, an apocalypse. Like a cyclone or a tornado, the encounter destroys everything in its path, overturns thoughts, habits, dreams, beliefs, everything that had allowed a man to hold himself up in this world. Who is able to love the disaster that will destroy them? Sauvage asked, with an accent of triumph I'd always associated with gamblers and traitors, I thought to myself, knowing that

nothing would turn him away now from his intentions. I
remember how he seemed proud of having revealed Cathie's
hidden face to me, a catastrophic face carrying memories of
disaster, he said, prouder still for having demonstrated that
I, who had believed himself to be cruel and who'd hoped to
see her again someday cured of my cruelness, was living either
in a false reality or in the depths of my own mental confusion. I'd pretended to be cruel, Sauvage reminded me, I'd
acted cruel when I was around her, remember how I'd gotten
caught up in my own little game, putting all my faith into
the power of my cruelty and ultimately deceiving myself
entirely. Cruelness is a lie, it had served as a barrier against
my fear and against the blackness of the night, he concluded
vehemently, and I did in fact think that with cruelty I could
avoid disaster, suddenly regretting my cruelty and considering that perhaps a cruel person is a man who is too cautious.
I still don't know what kind of secret revenge Sauvage was
nourishing as I began to show signs of despair after discovering the self-deception I'd been living in since leaving the
hospital. But I hold nothing against him, no, I don't even feel
I have the right to judge Sauvage after all that happened
between us. Cathie, he began again after a deep inhalation,
is one of those rare and fragile beings, the most attractive
kind of person whom we meet only once in our life, he said
again, and most often at the worst possible moment (of our
life), he thought it good to add, even at the moment when
it's impossible to bind yourself to her or begin any form of
relationship with her, a moment when no connection is possible, so that the encounter with this ideal other very quickly
turns into a disaster (as he said). Regarding encounters that
turn into pure and simple disasters, encounters which occur
at the very worst moment in the course of a human life and
more often than not brutally and permanently disrupt the
course of that life, giving it a radically new significance and
tonality, he had the most precise conceptions, which on that

evening, and for my benefit, he reduced to a simple and precisely formulated theory. We meet the ideal other only once in our life, Sauvage said, in the most improbable and unforeseeable of circumstances, and as soon as we've met her we tell ourselves that she's vital to our life and that we'll never be able to forget her, but more often than not we miss the train and find ourselves stranded on a platform, waiting in vain for years after the train has already left, not daring to leave our place out of fear that it might come again, and in the end, still standing in the same spot on the same platform, surrounded by indifferent travelers, we no longer even know what it is we're waiting for. But the opportunity is lost and we have no reason to be on the platform; our life hasn't changed and there's no change coming ever again, there won't be a second chance for bifurcation. Human behavior only allows a limited number of bifurcations and, in any case, he explained, these bifurcations rarely lead to anything of significance, most often they're just another dead end. We like to think that we're free to change our lives at any given moment, but when the chance for change presents itself we let it escape to some faraway place where it can never be recaptured, he said, and I wondered if I'd been dreaming the first time Cathie had smiled at me in the hospital, showing me an emergency exit in the long, neon-lit hallway of my existence. Was I already on the platform, had I already missed another train when I saw you, I asked myself, but then why smile at me, Cathie, why that smile that had filled me with so much false hope? I couldn't help but laugh at myself for my uncertainties. As I went on listening to him, I began to suspect that Sauvage's theory hid a secret wound he'd suffered in his life, or rather a missed opportunity, and that his theory could be judged in relation to his life and could probably even be qualified as a strictly personal theory; this is what I'd begun to think, and I laughed again at my doubts, my nagging doubts, which I felt like smashing against a wall.

Sauvage, I said to myself, had met the ideal other and had experienced the most powerful kind of attraction to her, but in the end he'd missed his opportunity with her. For him as well the meeting with the ideal other had ended in total failure, and he himself had waited on a platform filled with indifferent travelers occupied with their own concerns, who paid no attention to his suffering. When you meet her that one time in your life, you are already preparing to run away, he said later, and at first I hadn't understood why one would run away from what one loves, and I wondered why I would run away from you, Cathie, now that I know, and have no reason to doubt, what you meant for my life. Sauvage had himself experienced the disastrous consequences of an encounter, I said to myself, and his life had clearly fallen apart because of this failure, to such an extent that to this day he remained debilitated by the encounter, as incapable of recovering from the encounter as he was of honestly confronting its memory. And I tried to imagine the actions of the hopeless man who flees what he loves and then afterwards tries to forget his cowardice, and I said to myself that the man who so foolishly abandons what he loves or is ready to love must be a man who loves the death of love at least as much as love itself. This, then, is what I'd concluded, that at some moment in his life Sauvage had met the ideal other, the person who should have made him happy but had instead made him miserable, because he'd become frightened and had missed his opportunity with this person. He hadn't seized the chance when it had presented itself and he'd always regretted letting the opportunity slip away. His theory hid the essential, hid the untaken bifurcation, I said to myself then, it was his theory of consolation for life, for failure, for the things that can never be recaptured in a failed life. I had no doubts that his theory had been inspired by circumstances from his own life and so had to be put into perspective with those circumstances, circumstances located somewhere deep within his consciousness (and inaccessible to anybody but himself), circumstances that were nevertheless essential for a true understanding of Sauvage and Sauvage's life. Behind every theory, I said to myself, lies a hidden motive, and I would have given almost anything to know the motive hiding behind Sauvage's theory, because to know it would have been to no longer fear it. At that moment I was sure that every man was in some way a victim who had survived a disaster from which he would never fully recover and which filled him with dread every time he thought about it. Somewhere in Sauvage or in Sauvage's past dwelled the secret of his life, just as there dwells in every man and in his life the secret of his thoughts and his actions, a secret unlike any other, destined to remain unknown, especially to the man who unwittingly harbors it. And if I was now persuaded that Sauvage was a victim of some disaster who could only survive by denying a memory, I could also see that I myself was the miraculous survivor of a disaster who owed my life to nothing more than an instinctive refusal to let myself die. And what is true for Sauvage, I said to myself, must be true for every man, must be valid for everyone else, myself included. I knew that I'd met the ideal other, but something had stopped me from uniting with the true essence of her being, something so powerful and unfathomable that it outweighed the fear of a man facing his own death.

But my doubts were still lingering later in the evening, and I had more and more trouble persuading myself that Sauvage might be mistaken in thinking that all love leads to disaster and that every life founded on love is a failed existence. To be honest, I'd thought at first that in exposing me to his theory (which was not only personal but seemed to have been inspired entirely by events from his life) he'd wanted to confirm its universality by convincing me that I'd found the ideal other in Cathie, and that, without realizing it, I'd been in the presence of the person we meet once, and

only once, in our life. And I can't deny that I'd given in
without a trace of resistance to Sauvage's theory, accepting its
principles and its pessimistic consequences, taking it to be
true (I was in complete agreement) (following the example
of Sauvage) that every encounter is at its core and in almost
all of its qualities a non-encounter, or perhaps a kind of failed
encounter to such an extent that it can be qualified as a non-
encounter, or even a disaster. Because from the first day I'd
met Cathie, I'd truly believed that I was in a unique and
singular presence and that there was no other way for me to
view her than as an ideal human being. I was fascinated by
her kindness (the kindness of this ideal other) (who was no
doubt unique on earth) and I told myself that if the world is
capable of containing such people, I must adhere to this
world without reservation and do everything in my power to
accept it as it is, even if it's an imperfect world brimming over
with injustice. Cathie, I'd immediately understood (upon
meeting her), had faced life and the circumstances of her life
without anger and without regret, she'd grown up in this
imperfect world, which was also her own world, without the
thought of another world. She'd always lived without the
solace of a belief in another world, whereas I'd grown up
always thinking of another world, a world I was sure I could
join if I decided to make an effort, even if the most radical
and absolute means might be required to do so. The thought
of this world had always comforted me to some extent and,
during the moments when I no longer believed in my
potential in this world, I always felt stronger while thinking
of this inconsequential, nonexistent world. Had I met the
vital other? If that was the case, I also had to accept the
merciless conclusions of a theory that condemned my love
to failure. Had Cathie been, and was she still, my one chance
of salvation in this world? Yes, I'd no doubt glimpsed the vital
other in the likeness of Cathie and had loved her without
reservations, but I didn't want to believe that my chance with

this vital other (Cathie) was condemned to disaster. I didn't want to believe in disaster and I was ready to do everything in my power to refute Sauvage's theory; maybe, I thought, I am the living exception to the theory. I wasn't a victim of disaster and I would never share the miserable condition of a disaster victim, I said to myself, and at that moment I was ready to do anything to escape disaster, fear could no longer hold me back. Scientific theories (psychological theories included), Sauvage had alleged, are only valuable to the degree to which they allow us to confront the future, that is to say, allow us to predict in a rigorously precise manner the future of the species and the future of the individuals who make up the species. And I thought about my own future and asked myself if there was room for Cathie in this future, if there was still a chance for me to see her again. And that evening, I would say to Sauvage, emphatically, that I'd never left her, that she'd never left my thoughts, and that she'd always been with me. I'd made my decision, I added, and there was no turning back, I would see her again, tomorrow maybe, or perhaps next week, we'd never truly been apart to begin with. He hesitated before responding and then finally asked: Do you *honestly* think you will ever see her again? And then, as I was preparing my response, I understood that I would have to search far and long for her, far and long within myself, and that this time neither patience nor boldness would be enough to erase my uncertainty, I would have to find something else to beat back the doubt gnawing within me, I said to myself while noticing that the physiognomy of Sauvage had begun to darken, and I knew at once that he was going to announce something of great consequence, the perceptible change in his face made this clear. And now that Sauvage's jealousy was no longer a painfully hidden secret but a revelation that had exploded before our eyes, I said to myself that a body like his must house an insatiable curiosity, jealously guarded and condemned for eternity to live as a prisoner in his dungeon-like body, I said to myself again, a curiosity that he'd no doubt had great trouble concealing from the first day I met him but which was now exposed to the harsh light of day. Yes, I was planning to see her again and I'd already planned a meeting with her, I said with an air of defiance, without admitting to even myself that I was lying and without wondering if I really had any chance of seeing her again. Sauvage pretended not to hear me and (while removing his sunglasses) repeated his question: Do you honestly believe you will see her again? There was a trace of contempt in his eyes, or possibly of lust or some other vice (I was unsure if the object of his lust or contempt existed within himself or was part of the exterior world, the world common to us both), and he seemed to be addressing no one, or rather to be speaking only for himself, and because he'd asked the question a second time any possible response had been rendered futile. At that moment, I looked into his eyes, extremely clear and almost transparently blue, eyes like I'd never believed could exist on this earth, and in the waning light of the room, I don't know why, I became terrified by the thought that he might stand up. And in that same instant, as if it had sensed my fear and wanted to prevent my escape, his chair made a single bound and Sauvage was suddenly beside me, blocking the path to the door; but he was still seated and I tried to repress my fear by asking myself: Why would he possibly want to kill me now? But there was no reason for me to be afraid, I shouldn't even have been surprised. Sauvage had developed, it can be said without exaggeration, a close relationship with his chair, almost never getting out of it (at least in my presence), and he'd clearly discovered the most efficient ways to pivot and shift the chair exactly as he desired, with an economy of movement approaching the divine, able to maneuver himself with no apparent effort to any part of the room, precisely as if he'd recovered the usage of his legs. And I remembered that for weeks now the same scene had been repeated: as I entered the room I saw the unmoving shape of his shadow silhouetted by the small amount of light coming in through the window, and even before taking my designated chair, I noticed, without any idea how he'd so nimbly repositioned himself or how far he'd actually moved, that Sauvage's chair was already in a different place. And when I was at last facing Sauvage, under the dim light of the electric bulb, I found that I couldn't take my eyes off him, it was as if I wanted to assure myself that I wasn't being fooled by my senses, that the person before me was indeed Sauvage and not some escaped lunatic from the asylum. And I finally had to accept the fact that, in reality, Sauvage's armchair obeyed its own laws, following a trajectory (and speed) both unpredictable and irreversible. And Sauvage, I told myself, was neither the master nor owner of the armchair, as I'd first thought, but rather the helpless victim of its impulsive desires, and I imagined the chair to be endowed with a life of its own, made up of sudden turns and accelerations, a life with its own bifurcations that was not only a source of constant surprise for its occupant, but also a daily torment and trial. And on that day I'd again witnessed a sort of miracle, and as I thought this over I found myself feeling more and more alone and miserable, as if I'd been unworthy of witnessing what I'd seen, although I knew that one must always stand alone before a miracle, that no one else can be there at your side to witness it with you. And thinking of the miracle to which I'd been the sole and insufficient witness, I grew certain that the armchair had undergone a sudden death and would never move another millimeter. Sauvage's armchair, I said to myself, had reached the end of the course that had led Sauvage to the satisfaction of his curiosity, and I was certain, at that precise moment, facing the empty armchair that would never move again, I was certain, as I bent down to pick up the miniature Russian doll whose tiny round eyes watched me with manifest hatred, that I would never again try to find Cathie. Of that I was certain, and that was at least a start, I thought, facing the empty armchair.

SÉBASTIEN BREBEL was born in 1971 in Argenteuil, France. He lives in Nantes, where he teaches Philosophy, and is the author of three novels, of which this is his second to appear in English.

JESSE ANDERSON is a literary translator from Seattle. He has several forthcoming translations from Dalkey Archive Press, and his fiction and poetry have appeared in various literary journals and online.

MICHAL AJVAZ, *The Golden Age.*
  *The Other City.*

PIERRE ALBERT-BIROT, *Grabinoulor.*

YUZ ALESHKOVSKY, *Kangaroo.*

JOE AMATO, *Samuel Taylor's Last Night.*

ANTÓNIO LOBO ANTUNES, *Knowledge of Hell.*
  *The Splendor of Portugal.*

ALAIN ARIAS-MISSON, *Theatre of Incest.*

GABRIELA AVIGUR-ROTEM, *Heatwave and Crazy Birds.*

MIQUEL BAUÇÀ, *The Siege in the Room.*

ANDREI BITOV, *Pushkin House.*

ANDREJ BLATNIK, *You Do Understand.*
  *Law of Desire.*

LOUIS PAUL BOON, *Chapel Road.*
  *My Little War.*
  *Summer in Termuren.*

IGNÁCIO DE LOYOLA BRANDÃO,
  *Anonymous Celebrity.*
  *Zero.*

CHRISTINE BROOKE-ROSE,
  *Amalgamemnon.*

G. CABRERA INFANTE, *Infante's Inferno.*
  *Three Trapped Tigers.*

JULIETA CAMPOS, *The Fear of Losing Eurydice.*

ANNE CARSON, *Eros the Bittersweet.*

ORLY CASTEL-BLOOM, *Dolly City.*

LOUIS-FERDINAND CÉLINE, *North.*
  *Conversations with Professor Y.*
  *London Bridge.*

ERIC CHEVILLARD, *Demolishing Nisard.*
  *The Author and Me*

RENÉ CREVEL, *Putting My Foot in It.*

RALPH CUSACK, *Cadenza.*

NICHOLAS DELBANCO, *Sherbrookes.*
  *The Count of Concord.*

NIGEL DENNIS, *Cards of Identity.*

JEAN ECHENOZ, *Chopin's Move.*

LESLIE A. FIEDLER, *Love and Death in the American Novel.*

ANDY FITCH, *Pop Poetics.*

GUSTAVE FLAUBERT, *Bouvard and Pécuchet.*

MAX FRISCH, *I'm Not Stiller.*
  *Man in the Holocene.*

CARLOS FUENTES, *Christopher Unborn.*
  *Distant Relations.*
  *Terra Nostra.*

TAKEHIKO FUKUNAGA, *Flowers of Grass.*

PAULO EMÍLIO SALES GOMES, *P's Three Women.*

JUAN GOYTISOLO, *Count Julian.*
  *Juan the Landless.*

KEIZO HINO, *Isle of Dreams.*

KAZUSHI HOSAKA, *Plainsong.*

YORAM KANIUK, *Life on Sandpaper.*

ZURAB KARUMIDZE, *Dagny.*

JOHN KELLY, *From Out of the City.*

GEORGE KONRÁD, *The City Builder.*

TADEUSZ KONWICKI, *A Minor Apocalypse.*
  *The Polish Complex.*

ANNA KORDZAIA-SAMADASHVILI,
  *Me, Margarita.*

MENIS KOUMANDAREAS, *Koula.*

ELAINE KRAF, *The Princess of 72nd Street.*

JIM KRUSOE, *Iceland.*

AYSE KULIN, *Farewell: A Mansion in Occupied Istanbul.*

EMILIO LASCANO TEGUI, *On Elegance While Sleeping.*

ROSA LIKSOM, *Dark Paradise.*
YURI LOTMAN, *Non-Memoirs.*
HISAKI MATSUURA, *Triangle.*
ABDELWAHAB MEDDEB, *Talismano.*
ESHKOL NEVO, *Homesick.*
WILFRIDO D. NOLLEDO, *But for the Lovers.*

BORIS A. NOVAK, *The Master of Insomnia.*
CLAUDE OLLIER, *The Mise-en-Scène.*
*Wert and the Life Without End.*

FERNANDO DEL PASO, *News from the Empire.*
*Palinuro of Mexico.*

ROBERT PINGET, *The Inquisitory.*
*Mahu or The Material.*
*Trio.*

RAYMOND QUENEAU, *The Last Days.*
*Odile.*
*Pierrot Mon Ami.*
*Saint Glinglin.*

ANN QUIN, *Berg.*
*Passages.*
*Three.*
*Tripticks.*

JOÃO UBALDO RIBEIRO, *House of the Fortunate Buddhas.*

ALAIN ROBBE-GRILLET, *Project for a Revolution in New York.*
*A Sentimental Novel.*

ALIX CLEO ROUBAUD, *Alix's Journal.*
JACQUES ROUBAUD, *The Form of a City Changes Faster, Alas, Than the Human Heart.*
*The Great Fire of London.*
*Hortense in Exile.*
*Hortense Is Abducted.*
*Mathematics: A Novel*

TOMAŽ ŠALAMUN, *Soy Realidad.*
LUIS RAFAEL SÁNCHEZ, *Macho Camacho's Beat.*

STIG SÆTERBAKKEN, *Siamese.*
*Self-Control.*
*Through the Night.*

ARNO SCHMIDT, *Collected Novellas.*
*Collected Stories.*
*Nobodaddy's Children.*
*Two Novels.*

MARKO SOSIČ, *Ballerina, Ballerina*
GONÇALO M. TAVARES, *A Man: Klaus Klump.*
*Jerusalem.*
*Learning to Pray in the Age of Technique.*

MATI UNT, *Brecht at Night.*
*Diary of a Blood Donor.*
*Things in the Night.*

ÁLVARO URIBE & OLIVIA SEARS, EDS., *Best of Contemporary Mexican Fiction.*

ELOY URROZ, *Friction.*
*The Obstacles.*

JAY WRIGHT, *Polynomials and Pollen.*
*The Presentable Art of Reading Absence.*

PHILIP WYLIE, *Generation of Vipers.*
REYOUNG, *Unbabbling.*
VLADO ŽABOT, *The Succubus.*
ZORAN ŽIVKOVIĆ, *Hidden Camera.*
LOUIS ZUKOFSKY, *Collected Fiction.*
VITOMIL ZUPAN, *Minuet for Guitar.*
SCOTT ZWIREN, *God Head.*

*AND MORE . . .*